Oh, To Be a 'Cello

BOOKS BY BERT HORNBACK

Scenes from *The Dynasts* (1966)
The Metaphor of Chance (1971)
King Richard the Catsup (1971)
Noah's Arkitecture (1972)
The Norton Critical Edition of *Middlemarch* (1977)
The Hero of My Life: Essays on Dickens (1981)
An Annotated Bibliography for *Our Mutual Friend* (with Joel Brattin) (1985)
Great Expectations: A Novel of Friendship (1988)
Middlemarch: A Novel of Reform (1989)
Bright Unequivocal Eye (2000)
The Norton Critical Edition of *Middlemarch (2nd edition)* (2000)
Talking About Poetry (2002)
The Ideal of Tragedy (2003)
The Wisdom in Words (2004)
The Wisdom in Words (2nd edition) (2006)
Grimwig: A Novel (2012)
Bert Borrone's Perpetual Motion: A Memoir (2013)
Anemones My Footstool (forthcoming)

Oh, To Be a 'Cello

Bert Hornback

PORTLAND • OREGON
INKWATERPRESS.COM

Scan this QR Code to learn more about this title.

Cover and interior design by Jayme Vincent

Classical Cello Isolated On White Background with Musical Notes © Nahariyani. Shutter-Stock.com

Publisher: Inkwater Press | www.inkwaterpress.com

Paperback
ISBN-13 978-1-62901-219-3 | ISBN-10 1-62901-219-X

Printed in the U.S.A.

1 3 5 7 9 10 8 6 4 2

For
Kathleen Lyons

CONTENTS

PREFACE

This little book has happened in pieces over the course of a number of years. None of the pieces ever thought of being part of a book; they were occasional pieces. They came together because they are all in some way about music.

Most of them are essays of one sort or another. The title piece was delivered as a lecture to the University of Michigan Musical Society in Ann Arbor, Michigan, preliminary to a concert by Yo-Yo Ma. "Four Hands" was written in memory of Otto and Sarah Graf, and first published in the University of Michigan *Alumnus.* "Mozart at St. Paul's" originally appeared in a slightly different form in *Notre Dame* magazine. "The Washington Post March" is reprinted from the Western Kentucky University *Alumni Magazine.* "Mr. Leopold Bloom Determines (Tentatively) to Learn the Blowbags" first appeared in *James Joyce Studies,* published with *The Abiko Quarterly.*

Words that Sing, the second part of this book, is made up of various pieces of music that have come to me over the years. Generously, four students—now colleagues—helped me put them together, perform them, and write them down. I am deeply indebted to Chris Carter, Devon Hershey, Patrick Kutscha, and most recently Jan Paulus, for all the work they did for and with me.

"A Classical Round" is the product of a whimsical inspiration experienced one summer while driving to an American Youth Foundation camp on Lake Michigan; when I arrived at my destination and tried it out with Bud Brewster and two other friends, it worked! It is a silly little appreciation of J. S. Bach, Mozart, Beethoven, and Brahms.

The other pieces of music are several poems which while living in my head over many years have found their way into songs. Poems, after all, were meant to be sung—and have been, since Homer's time, and King David's. An ode is a Greek song. A sonnet is what a musician would call a sonata—and the musician wouldn't make up any nonsensical rules it was supposed to abide by! Lyrics aren't just the words to songs: "lyric" comes from the musical instrument, the *lyre,* which accompanies the words being sung.

I haven't looked for these melodies; they have come to me of their own accord—even the long ones like those for Thomas Hardy's "To an Unborn Pauper Child" and William Wordsworth's "Ode: Intimations of Immortality from Recollections of Early Childhood." The various melodies belong more to the poets whose work they represent than they do to me. I have performed them occasionally, and have sung them all in concert, first in Louisville, Kentucky, then in Ann Arbor, and most recently in Saarbrücken, Germany.

Music exists in this world, not just as performance, and certainly not as publication. It is experience, a constant, complex motion in the world of pleasure. At the end of one of the greatest songs in Western literature, the "Ode: Intimations of Immortality," Wordsworth writes of "Thoughts that do often lie too deep for tears." Those are musical thoughts, surely, musical imaginings, what William Butler Yeats says he can "hear . . . in the deep heart's core." They are what Seamus Heaney pleads for when he asks David Hammond, in "The Singer's House," to "raise it again, man"—because "we still believe what we hear."

Some years ago I was sitting with my mother in the nursing home where she lived, and where I visited with her every afternoon. There was a music program in the parlor, organised by several of the residents, to honor the Fourth of July. The recorded offerings were all Sousa marches. As my mother and I swung our feet and hummed along, our lives together melted into smiles and glistening eyes. What we were remembering wasn't important, though we surely had the same generic experience of music—Sousa's and otherwise—swelling in our throats and filling our hearts: affirming our love. What I saw in the sound of Soua's marches and in the brightness of my mother's eyes is in the little piece which appears here as "The Washington Post March."

Music *is* an affirmation. And I offer you these little pieces about music and the poems set to music in celebration of that affirmation.

Bert Hornback

Saarbrücken, Germany
April 2015

MOZART AT ST. PAUL'S

First it was a finger in his mouth. Then two, thumb and index finger. Then it was most of a small fist. He worked with decorum, almost with piety.

If there is a liturgy for the pulling of a last baby molar during the sermon at St. Paul's, he was following it. If there wasn't such a liturgy, he invented it that day.

And it was timed to the sermon, perfectly. Just before the blessing with which the sermon ended, he produced the tooth, held it in his right hand, delicately, bloodily, his left hand cupped protectively underneath. And his face glowed with heavenly triumph.

I had been to St. Paul's for three straight Sundays. It was July. I had just finished my summer teaching for the University of Michigan, an annual program that let me take a dozen students to England and Ireland for ten weeks. We ended our trip each year in London. I usually stayed on for a few weeks, to relax and recuperate and enjoy the city. And one of favorite enjoyments in London has long been St. Paul's and its music.

As usual, that summer I had heard, on successive Sunday mornings, Mozart's *Missa Brevis,* Hayden's *Nelson Mass,* and the Schubert Mass in B. When I was growing up, Catholics "heard mass." But we never heard mass the way you hear it at St. Paul's!

I had been to evensong, too, maybe six or ten times during those three weeks. The men's and boys' voices, *a capella* in that great ornate *capella* that Christopher Wren built to challenge Michelangelo.

The men in the choir didn't change. During the twenty years I had been a summer regular at St. Paul's I had seen very few changes in the men's section. But the boys changed. Though I learned every one of those twenty-four faces every summer, they all seemed new and different a year later. And some of them were, of course. They had grown a year older: some had grown up, their voices had changed and they were gone. Some of those trebles from now more than twenty years ago are middle-aged men. Their sons may well be among the breath-voiced boys singing at St. Paul's this year.

For evensong I always sat in the choir stalls. On Sundays I sat under the dome, on the front row, dead center on the left side, which put me right in the middle of the orchestra and choir. That was I could hear both the choir and the individual voices—and I was close enough to see the boys' faces.

The more exotic boys were usually situated at the ends of the rows. They moved about like young rock stars, or saucy birds in red cassocks and surplices. They counterpointed decorum, and added a human dimension to angelic sound.

That year the head angel at St. Paul's was a red-haired boy. I didn't remember a red-haired boy from the year before, but he must have been there—and for at least four years before that. But I hadn't noticed him before.

He was a magnet, however, his carroty top and pale face an ecclestical decoration conferred by nature, and reverenced by all the other boys.

Though I couldn't help looking at him, I couldn't differentiate his voice from all the others. I could hear the silver bells, and identify them: they belonged to plainer, simpler, younger faces. Vocally, the red-haired head boy was just a chorister. But he was head boy, and wore in addition to his red hair a big gold medallion suspended around his neck on a wide red ribbon.

The last Sunday of July was, as usual, Mozart's *Coronation Mass,* which is maybe the most beautiful, moving, exalted thing I have ever known. Not a thing, of course—and not an experience, nothing so clichéd as that. A non-thing, perhaps, a divine vacuum of perfection, a stilling transcendence, a magic crown of soaring harmonies and clear single notes that rise beyond harmony.

The sermon was human, always, and an interruption. When Bishop Woollcombe used to preach that mass, he always preached on Mozart—as though Mozart were the God, or the creator of the God.

But it wasn't Bishop Woolcombe that Sunday. I don't remember who it was. My attention was focused on my red-haired treble, sitting importantly in the middle of the front row of the choir, holding—by the end of the sermon—his freshly excavated tooth out in front of him.

The other boys—twenty-three admiring, astonished young faces—turned full upon him. Or turned, rather, upon the hand that held the bloody little molar.

The preacher left the high pulpit. The orchestra lifted instruments from knees, bent ears to test strings, raised bows. 'Cellos to the ready; violins under chins.

The conductor stood, turned, and looked thoughtfully at his music. My young red-haired hero held out his hands as thogh he held an offering, or a miracle. A triumph, to be incensed or applauded.

We were ready for Mozart's great Credo. The conductor lifted his head, and at the same time raised his hands to raise his choir.

They stood. And in the middle of the front row, in red cassock and white surplice, a gleaming gold medallion suspended around his neck and down his front on a rich red velvet ribbon, stood my red-haired transitional angel with his bloody prize extended before him.

The conductor looked. I couldn't see his face, of course. I only saw his right arm extend in a dramatic gesture, his index finger pointing. "Go," the pointing hand said.

The head chorister bowed a small, decorous bow, and paraded in miniature dignity—as though being led by a wandsman—across and out.

When he was gone, and the enraptured eyes of the innocents had returned to this world, the conductor raised his baton. For Mozart, and God.

At the end of the credo the hero rejoined the choir, solemn-faced, eyes lowered, his hands clasped humbly below his waist. He bowed gently, and resumed his seat.

Then, grinning like a miracle-worker for all the faithful, he elevated the washed and gleaming molar for the edification of his peers.

We all stood, then—four thousand of us—and sang the offertory hymn.

GREAT THINGS

They didn't sing it. They said it, recited it from the tiny balcony of their room on Pembroke Road in Dublin. I was there for the premier performance. It was 17 June, 1978. It was just a week before David's twentieth birthday.

It wasn't a poem I knew, or knew well. It wasn't part of our syllabus for the summer study course that had let me bring them first to Englsnd and now to Ireland that summer. David had found it, reading through the *Collected Poems* of Thomas Hardy, and had persuaded Mark to learn it with him.

And there they were, the two of them, out on that little two-feet deep balcony of our Georgian bed and breakfast on Pembroke Road. Giggly at first. But then they started.

"Great Things"

by
Thomas Hardy

Sweet cyder is a great thing,
A great thing to me,
Spinning down to Weymouth town
By Ridgeway thirstily,
And maid and mistess summoning
Who tend the hostelry:
O cyder is a great thing,
A great thing to me!

Pembroke Road isn't a busy street, but there were a few people passing. They stopped, and listened.

The dance it is a great thing,
A great thing to me,
With candles lit and partners fit
For night-long revelry;
And going home when day-dawning
Peeps pale upon the lea:
O dancing is a great thing,
A great thing to me!

By the third verse there were maybe twenty people listening. We were an audience.

Love is, yea, a great thing,
A great thing to me,
When, having drawn across the lawn
In darkness silently,
A figure flits like one a wing
Out from the nearest tree:
O love is, yea, a great thing,
A great thing to me!

A happy poem, about "great things." The old man, remembering and affirming. Hardy was nearly eighty—my age now—when he wrote it.

Will these be always great things,
Great things to me? . . .
Let it befall that One will call,
'Soul, I have need of thee:'
What then? Joy-jaunts, impassioned flings,
Love, and its ecstacy,
Will always have been great things,
Great things to me!

Clear, straightforward. Yes. "Great things." Always. We applauded, nodded, smiled. Yes.

And like Dutch boys on a weather-clock, David and Mark popped back into their room, waited a few minutes, and were out again.

Sweet cyder is a great thing,
A great thing to me . . .

I hadn't occasion to recite the poem, myself, for four years after that. I had added it to the syllabus for the England and Ireland summer program, to be sure. And in my head I saw David and Mark on their little balcony in Dublin every time we read it or talked about it. It was their song. And I usually told kids about David and Mark, on Pembroke Road.

Three years after their summer trip, in 1981, Gregg Benjamins liked "Great Things" a lot. It surprised me. Gregg was a serious young man who didn't have much room in his life for nonsense or silliness—or cyder, I would have thought. But he liked "Great Things."

When classes resumed at the University of Michigan that fall Gregg and I began to work together on his senior Honors thesis on Hardy. He was making good progress, but working at the other end of Hardy's sense of the world from the one you get in "Great Things." The line Gregg was using to grow his ideas was from *Tess of the D'Urbervilles:* "Experience is as to intensity, and not as to duration."

On the first day of classes in January of 1982—on the first day of his last term in college—Gregg became suddenly ill, and died within hours. He was twenty-two.

I had known Gregg since the beginning of his freshman year. I remember his first day's in-class "scribble": "So this is the great Professor Hornback. Well, we'll see if he is such." He was my student both terms that year, and reappeared in the fall of his sophomore year. We studied together again in his junior year, and then he joined the summer trip. I knew him well.

I planned to go to Montague, Michigan, for the memorial service the Saturday after Gregg died. Most of his friends went up on Friday; I was going to drive up on Saturday morning early, and bring along several more students. Overnight there was a major blizzard, and by dawn on Saturday the roads north of Lansing were all closed.

Ruth and Ed Benjamins ended up with seventeen of Gregg's friends in their house that weekend. There wasn't a memorial service—or at any rate not the one that they had planned, at the local church. But for three days Ed and Ruth and Gregg's friends memorialised him. Remembered him. Loved him.

When the spring thaw came in April, Ruth wrote to ask me to come up for Gregg's funeral. His ashes were to be buried in the little cemetery overlooking Lake Michigan. They asked me if I would say something at the funeral.

I had written Ruth and Ed what I wanted to say about Gregg right after he died, and had given it to them when they left Ann Arbor, to take him home. There wasn't anything more or other that I wanted to say—so I read some Hardy for him. For us.

The last thing I read was "Great Things." And when I finished, and looked up at his tombstone, it occurred to me that what Hardy says about life in "Great Things" is not at all unlike what he said in the line from *Tess* that Gregg liked so much. The tone is different, but the idea is the same.

"Experience is as to intensity and not as to duration" is what it says on Gregg's tombstone. A distillation. I wish there were room for "Great Things" there, too! The full music, even though the life was short.

"THE ARCHERS"

Dum-dum-de-doodle-de-dum,
Dum-dum-de-doodle-de-dum . . . .

We were in Goldie's bar, in Dorchester, in the Southwest of England. I used to visit there every year on my summer trip with students—it's the center of Thomas Hardy country—and over the years I had made some friends. Andy was an artist, and a very good one; he exhibited regularly in the Royal Academy's big summer show. Elisabeth, his wife, had been a superb ballerina, and was then teaching dancing. (That's English culture: a small county town can have a noted ballerina giving lessons.) Phil was the Thursday editor of *The Guardian* in London; he came down by train every weekend. John and Jean were antique dealers—and career anti-nuclear activists. We met once a year, for the weekend, in Goldie's. And we had serious conversations.

We also had lots of fun.

Goldie's doesn't hold many people. It is a low-ceilinged Tudor house, with four small tables and a nook in the bay window so old that it is allowed to stand with historical impunity well out into the sidewalk. At the bar there are five or six stools.

One year on our Saturday night there was a slightly drunken little man sitting in the middle of the room, his small bald head bright in the heavy smoke. His girlfriend, considerably larger than he was, seemed in charge. Every so often she bought him another pint and herself another schnapps.

Nobody was ever loud in Goldie's, though sometimes the punch-line of a joke would get repeated half a dozen times across the room. And sometimes, after five or six pints, Phil would croon the first line of "Moon River"—and then talk about how much he liked jazz.

Andy was the one who really liked—and knew—jazz. One summer he and Elisabeth were gone for most of my weekend because there was a jazz combo playing in a pub in Bristol that Andy needed to hear.

But this isn't about jazz, or Andy or Phil or John and Jean. It's about Joe, the little fellow with the bald head and the big girlfriend.

I don't know what got Joe started. I had seen him before, and the rest of us always said hello to him and his girlfriend. But they had never been part of our conversations, nor us a part of theirs. Joe was just one of the middle-of-the-room drinkers—like us, except when we got to Goldie's early enough to get the nook in the bay window.

Joe was a regular at Goldie's. And not other than a wise man, I guess. He won the Sunday night bar quiz once when I was there, and nobody seemed surprised. Current events, recent history, sports, culture. Joe knew a lot.

The Archers had already been on radio in England for more than forty years. Everybody knew them. Infants were born in Britain already knowing the theme music for *The Archers.* I'm not sure that anybody ever listened to the program—I've never met a listener, or heard anybody talk about what was happening to whom. But everybody knew them—or knew, at least, the theme music that introduced them five days a week.

So that year, in Goildie's pub, completely out of any kind of context and for no reason at all, Joe started singing it. *"Boop-boop-de-boodle-de-boop, Boop-boop-de-boodle-de-boop."* His shoulders swung a bit as he sang, and he sort of pumped his arms. His wrists flicked.

Everybody looked his way, and he did it again. He had a skinny, nasal voice, but it was pitched true: he could carry a tune.

"Tup-tup-de-tootle-de-tup, Tup-tup-de-tootle-de-tup."

Joe was an ex-soldier. He had spent twenty-odd years in the British Army, repairing lorries and tanks and motorcycles. He valued what he did, and didn't regret the army. It put him where he was, he said: driving a lorry, repairing big diesels, sitting in Goldies drinking a few pints. And singing—for no reason at all, as far as we could tell—the theme from *The Archers.*

"It's the fucking best tune there is in Britain," he said to everybody. "I mean, that's the tune to pick the country up. Never mind all these schemes from London and all the par-li-men-tar-fucking-y programs and schemes. You couldn't goose a turkey with that stuff."

Joe looked around for approval. He got it—or got silence, at least. Bemused silence, at the quiet member's speech.

"So," he said after a bit. He didn't give us time to start talking again, just time to think about talking again, going on with the evening.

"So what do we do? We change the fucking national fucking anthem. That "God Save Our Noble Queen" stuff. It's about as musical as blowing your nose in church. About as bloody up-lifting, too!" He eyed us all, daring disagreement.

"So we'll get a new one. *Boop-boop-de-boopity-boop, Boop-boop-de-boopity-boop!* Right, mates?"

Joe raised his boney little shoulders a bit, and sort of pumped his arms as he looked around the room. But nobody was paying any attention now. It had passed, and we were back to our usual conversations.

Phil had had enough pints to want to sing the first line of "Moon River," and we all laughed at him. Goldie's nasty little dog barked, and it was time to go home.

The next year when I came back to Dorchester, I headed off first thing for Goldie's—as usual. It was just after the afternoon lockdown, and the pub was open again. Andy was already there, perched on a stool in one corner of the short bar, nursing a pint of bitter and pretending not to smoke. Goldie was behind the bar. I said hello, and settled in next to Andy and his pint. We chatted our affirmations that the world hadn't changed—George Bush's bloody war, Thatcher's fall, famine in Africa, unemployment, greed. Same world. The usual. And thank God for the Germans: yes.

And then I saw Joe, sitting there wearing the same bald head and across the table from the same large woman.

I went over and tapped him on the off shoulder. *"Dum-dum-de-dum-de-dum,"* I sang.

They both looked up. "Hey," she said. "I remember you. That was last year—last year in here!"

Joe looked at me and nodded a firm, serious nod.

"That's right, ain't it? Fucking change this fucking world with that one."

He didn't smile, at first. Just looked me in the eye.

"It's worth a try," I said.

Joe nodded again. And he grinned a tough little grin. "Fucking change this fucking world."

And he was off. He sang it, his shoulders waving like the Atlantic, his arms pumping loosely, his elbows doing little *risque* tricks.

"*Boop-boop-de-boop-de-boop. Boop-boop-de-boop-de-boop.* Can you imagine sending a bunch of kids off to war—getting them to line up to go get killed, marching to that one?"

He shook his head, and smiled, knowingly. "Or the Queen. Can you figure this fucking country supporting all those royals—how much do they pay her a year to be queen? Three hundred million is it?"

"Listen. If every time she came into the room, everybody had to stand up and do a few rounds of *Boop-boop-de-boop-de-boop,* they'd catch on, wouldn't they? And they would cut her off without a penny."

I agreed.

But Joe wasn't finished. He'd been thinking about it—all year, perhaps.

"*Boop-boop-de-boop-de-boop.*"

I took it up with him for the repeat, and he stuck out his hand. We wagged our hands together, and went on to the third line: *Boop-boop-de-boop-de-boop-de poop-py.*"

"You're a genius, Joe," I said admiringly.

"We could fucking change this fucking world."

"We could."

"They'd all get their heads up. And their tails up. And they'd look around them And they'd be so fucking happy."

I was getting almost misty-eyed, dreaming Joe's dream. But Joe wasn't. He stopped my hand, and loosed his. He looked down into his pint. He picked it up, and tilted the flat beer around inside the big glass.

"Fuck it. Those bleedy bastards won't listen to Joe. Who's he? Never heard of him Nothing doing."

When I left Goldie's that afternoon I walked down the High Street, doing "The Archers" theme in my head. But it wouldn't work. It was more like a dirge. My feet were heavy, and my elbows were just ordinary, everyday old elbows. No music, no dance in them at all.

And that was years and years before Mr. Obama and his drones.

INCIDENTAL MUSIC

I have always been fond of flags. They make me think of bands, and marching. When I was little I would tie a handkerchief or a dinner napkin to a stick, and march around singing. Since then, I have made several more serious flags, all associated incidentally with music. Which is my excuse for writing about them.

When I was briefly a Boy Scout, I designed the flag for my patrol. It featured a toga-clad buffalo with a wreath of olives around its head. We were the Roman Buffalo Patrol. And our patrol's marching song was, of course, "Home on the Range" But when our scoutmaster saw our flag, he vetoed it, and us. He wouldn't allow us to be Roman Buffalos. Buffalos, he said, were American, and they *roamed*. So I gave up on scouting.

Later in life—at twenty-one instead of twelve—I made a flag for my platoon of U. S. Marine lieutenants while were were in Basic School at Quantico, Virginia. All the platoons had marching songs, and ours—over loud objections from our smallest lieutenant—was "Mickey Mouse." I made us a big-eared Mickey Mouse flag to carry—and submitted the names of all forty-four of us for membership in the Mickey Mouse Club. We were duly announced as members on television.

Our captain wouldn't let us carry my flag when we marched—but he didn't make us stop singing our song, or object the mouse-ears we put up over the doors to the quonset hut where we lived.

My best flag was a lovely blue one, with a big yellow banana and a scattering of handsome silver stars. It was meant to be sung to, of course, and saluted. It flew in front of my house in Louisville, Kentucky, until my neighbors realised what it was and took it down for me one night. It was the Star-Spanglid Banana.

I didn't invent the Star-Spangled Banana. Jim Bergquist did that. He was the program director for the student radio station at the University of Notre Dame when I was there. And every morning when we went on the air and every night when we signed off, we played what Jim called the Star-Spangled Banana.

Notre Dame had a famous school song—called a "fight song," of course. Notre Dame was a Catholic school, dedicated to Jesus's mother—and Jesus was a pacifist. But we had a fight song, and the Notre Dame football team was (and still is) called "the Fighting Irish."

Cheer, cheer, for old Notre Dame!

A group of my fellow-students and I decided to sing in English, and using our native tongue sang

Cheer, cheer, for our old lady!

But our classmates didn't like that, and said it was disrespectful and a mockery of what our university stood for. And anyway, we often arrived late for football games, and sometimes left early.

One of my friends at Notre Dame had been his high school's cheer-leader. Boys weren't supposed to be cheer-leaders, but Walter was. And as he was big and shaved twice a week by the time he was sixteen, it was okay for him to be one. And he wrote his school's fight song. Springfield High School didn't have a school song till he gave it one. The song had a simple melody—a melody so simple it wasn't a melody. Except for the last two words of the second and fourth lines, which went down the scale, it was all sung on one note.

Springfield High School
You're sure a good school.
Rah! Rah!
Springfield High School.
Good school.
Rah! Rah!

It was more like a dirge than a fight song, but the kids in his school loved it. And it made kids at other schools either angry or jealous.

Americans in those days were always singing the Star-Spangled Banner. No real sports event could happen without such. At the height of the Vietnam War, a young man (with connections) was singing the Star-Spangled Banner at Kiel Auditorium in St. Louis. and he got so involved in its violence that after

O say can you see
By the dawn's early light
What so proudly we hailed
At the twilight's last gleaming

and then—forgetting about "Whose broad stripes and bright stars," the "perilous night," and the "ramparts"—he "jumped the gun," as they say in America, and sang

And the rockets red glare—

and then

And the rockets red glare
And the rockets red glare
And the rockets red glare

until finally he got to

And the rockets red glare,
The bombs bursting in air

but by then the audience of maybe 12,000 people was laughing riotously, and nobody heard the rest of it, about

The land of the free,
And the home of the brave.

There were too many bombs for that.

A New York radio station had Paul Simon in its studio one night during its live marathon support drive. Somebody called in and offered to give a thousand dollars if Paul Simon would sing along with Kate Smith on "God Bless America." And though Kate Smith was a long-time patriotic idol who had sung the "God Bless America" a million times, the station didn't have a record with her singing it. But somebody sent one by taxi, and the station played it. And Paul Simon sang along with Kate Smith.

Two and a half glorious minutes. Then it started over. Two and a half minutes more. And again, Simon and Smith singing together. Again, with drum rolls. Then with sound effects—bombs going off—and Simon giggling, laughing. More. And again, bombs whistling and big explosions. Near hysteria from Simon.

Then the announcer's voice: "It will take another thousand dollars to make this stop."

It was so painful, the donations flooded in, and the whole thing was over.

For years I taught for two weeks every summer at a camp for 17-21 year olds. It was a camp sponsored by the Christian-oriented American Youth Foundation. One summer in the 1970s I was the faculty sponsor for the graduating class of young men. I listened as they planned their graduation ceremony, to be held at the open-sided non-denominational Church of the Dunes, high up and overlooking Lake Michigan. The young men chose decent love-your neighbor, pacific readings from the Christian bible, few nice hymns, a kiss of peace, and then—as a recessional, to march to as they left the Church—"Onward Christian Soldiers, Marching as to War."

I explained to them that if they sang that, I would get up and throw myself over the railing and roll down the dune screaming.

At their graduation, they walked out singing "Let there be peace on earth, and let in begin with me." And I followed them.

Incidental music. Little bits, perhaps, from the music of the spheres, falling down occasionally to enliven things. Or little bits of cacophony. Or little bits of cacaphony. But musical, still.

FOOT-DANCING

If you weigh two hundred and twenty pounds—as I once did—it's hard to dance the kind of flinging, air-raising affirmations that you dream of when the squeeze-box and the tin whistle start, and the bothran does its double-thump between your ears.

And you can't just tap your toes to Irish music. It asks more of you than that. Even if there aren't any young girls out there on the floor like high-speed sparrows doing the bunny hop, and boys hammering the hooley, a bunch of beardless, freckled goats with big-booted magic feet. And a stern-faced old fellow off to the side, solo, woodpeckering away at the boards non-stop for hours.

There was a time when I would attempt it, pathetically. But at two hundred and twenty pounds, defying gravity was as silly as Lucifer's pretense at freedom, or the Easter Rebellion. And even I couldn't pretend to see any terrible beauty in my dance.

I could do the steps, and with some precision even. But the diver springs before he does his flip, the vaulter goes up before he comes down. And my dance was all down. Every time one leg went out, I pegged it closer to the floor. And though Ireland is—or was—Catholic, the limbo isn't an Irish dance.

Irish dancing is not just dancing, or simply exercise. It is indeed exercise—fast exercise—but it is as lyrical as anything the quick-witted gods have ever dreamed of. Even angels sweat when they dance in Ireland, and their feet get heavy trying to keep up with the locals.

What I did, trying to dance, was Quince to the *nth.* Frustrated by my gross and grotesque failure, I gave up. I kept my to my seat, in sympathetic but defeated dignity. I learned to flex my thigh muscles secretly, making them do the dancing, with nothing to support but my mind. And the thigh muscles proved adequate for that. Jigs and reels, a whole evening of jigs and reels, shut-eyed, the silly mind believing itself afloat, graced, flying, doing ceoli touchdowns and overs.

But lately—some pounds taken off and old age coming on and with it a slyer wisdom, maybe—I've developed farther. I'm a foot-dancer now. These days, I sit at my table, wise, private, decorous, happy, and straight up, sitting as tall as I can, my bottom securely planted and my legs—from the knees down—free and light, ready for the music to start.

My right foot does the rhythm work, the bothran, for the most part. My left foot sings—descants ecstatically, pampooties exotic and impossible steps, dares the musicians to play faster and faster.

Dancers on the floor wilt, retire in exhaustion. Are replaced. The old fellow woodpeckers on. Freckled boys sweat their freckles off. Girls with feet of ether materialise again, come down, stand, laugh, sigh. I keep dancing, dancing.

My right foot, emboldened to competition, does a double-thump, tilts its heel, teasing, proposing. My left foot plays along, encouurages, throws a heel-kiss. Down the line, then, and through the set. Next time—next time . . .

Kiss!

The right foot thumps, *yes!*—but the left foot laughs, is off again, dancing, pucking the air, the floor, the music in between. Affirming the music, more than the kiss.

Eventually, of course, the music stops, the evening's done. Even Irish music stops, but only after eternity has been defined.

Ceoli. That's the Irish word for music, dance. *Caelo,* or *Caelum*: that's holy Latin—I remember it from the old Latin church. It's the word for the heavens. And Irish dancing: that's "*Ceoil Caelorum*"—the music of the heavens, the music of the spheres. And this body of mine knows that, experiences it, foot-dancing under the table.

FOUR HANDS

Sarah was a fat little girl from Sioux City. She came running into my head the other day at a shoe store in Saarbrücken, Germany. I wanted a pair of fancy dress moccasins called "Sioux." When I asked for them the clerk gave me a curious look. "Ein moccasin," I said. "Ah!"—and he pronounced all the letters: "Sooks," he said.

Sarah from Sioux City was born just over a hundred years ago. Her father ran a junk yard; she was a pianist. Everybody in Sioux City knew about the fat little girl whose father spoke Yiddish. She played everywhere, places where her father couldn't have gone even if he hadn't run a junk yard. Sioux City had never known or heard or seen or dreamed of such a musician as Sarah Weiner was.

The fat little girl from Sioux City went to Ann Arbor in 1928, to study piano at the University of Michigan. One day in her Shakespeare class she wrote her name and campus address in the book of the boy who sat next to her. And they got married.

Otto was a pianist, too. He came from Indianapolis. His piano teacher there had recommended a teacher in Detroit, so after high school Otto had enrolled at the Universuity of Michigan, and commuted by bus once a week to Detroit for his lesson.

Otto and Sarah Graf stayed on in Ann Arbor after they graduated. Otto went on to do his doctoratre in German, and joined the faculty of the university. Sarah lost weight, began to dance, and played the lead in a dozen shows for the Nell Gwynn Players. Otto was their orchestra.

I first met Otto at the university in the late 1960s. He was a professor of German, and the director of the Honors Program. I might have guessed, that afternoon, that he was a professor of Music, or of Japanese. We had an interesting conversation, and he asked with what I thought of as old-world politeness if I would do him the honor of stopping by his office for a more comfortable chat.

I met Sarah a few months later, in the music room of their home. She was a tiny woman with a wonderful grey Afro, and the eyes of a very bright mouse. She wore a black cocktail dress, and a black velvet band around her neck. She was the center of attention for everybody—including Otto.

The occasioin was one of the Grafs' musical afternoons, concerts which Sarah and Otto gave twice a year for their friends—and Sarah's piano students and their parents.

There were maybe thirty of us crowded into the music room on three rows of folding chairs. Another half-dozen or so sat on the stairs, and a few rude and ignorant husbands adjourned to the kitchen to have a drink.

The two big Steinways nuzzled each other in the music room. Sarah's was shiny, like an elegsant black mirror.

I cried, listening to them play. This, I thought, was civilisation.

The Grafs and I became friends. We sort of adopted each other as family. Soon Otto and I worked together in the Honors Program, and I used its office as my office, not my office in Haven Hall.

And Sarah became my piano teacher.

I had wanted to play the piano since I was three years old. The Hornbacks lived with my mother's parents—and two sisters and a brother—that year, while what was to be our house was being built. My mother was an excellent pianist, and loved to play. The year we lived with the Borrones there was always music in the house, except during Grandad's and my afternoon naps.

When we moved into our house, my mother and I stopped by the big old house on College Street almost every day, and my mother would play. And I played, too. I would pick out melodies that I knew, make up tunes on my own. Sometimes I would experiment with two keys at one time, testing harmonies.

Once I started school, we would stop at the Borrones' on the way home. When I was in fourth grade I got to take piano lessons at school, and then we had to stop by every afternoon, so I could practice. And I could practice, Gran said, even if Grandad was taking his nap.

In college I always said I was going to take lessons again. But I never did, even though I ached with love and envy every time I heard somebody play.

And without intending fraud, I learned to strum my fingers on the table or in the air as though I were playing.

For Sarah's seventieth birthday I gave me a piano, and asked her to be my teacher. And for four years I practiced, and learned to play a few small things.

I played them well—musically—because Sarah wouldn't accept anything else.

But after those four years I quit taking lessons. And at about the same time the music at the Grafs' stopped. Not because of me, but because Saerah and Otto were getting old, suddenly, and tired. First the concerts stopped. Then Otto's arthritis in his hands made him stop playing. Then Sarah stopped giving lessons.

We would talk about music when I visited, which was almost every afternoon. They talked music by the hour, stting there in the kitchen through the dreary winter, things collecting on ther table. In the summer, too, when the doors were open and fresh air blew through the house.

Or they listened to the radio. To music on the radio.

Otto and Sarah didn't move about much in those days. They sat in the kitchen together, most of the time. The five steps down to the music room were dangerous, and hard to manage.

The two pianos were still tuned, but only the tuner played them. And the callouses on the tips of Sarah's short, blunt fingers softened and disappeared.

Now I was listening to the radio—to the finals of the Dublin International Piano Competition, broadcast live from the National Concert Hall. The finalists were—are—six young pianists in their twenties, from Russia and Italy and Brazil and Japan. And two from America.

The one I am listening to is young Otto Graf, from Indianapolis, Indiana. But also a German, of course: his parents were from Hanover. Listening, I see him. His shoulders are hunched forward because I have never seen him otherwise, never having known him when he was straight-backed, erect. He plays wuith elegance that is natural, not studied. It is Beethoven's "Emperor." He nods to himself every now and then, or to his conductor. When he concludes he will judge his own performance—is judging it as he plays, and judging too the piano and the orchestra and the conductor and the audience.

And Sarah, from Sioux City. She plays next. She is the beautiful little Sarah I have known, only younger. Much younger. She is the Sarah of the picture that used to sit on Otto's desk. She sits upright, like a small bird, perched before the concert grand, her feet hanging perfectly still, her head tilted slightly toward the conductor. She is as still as a piece of crystal.

It is Tchaikovski's first that she will play. I hold my breath. It will be—superb!

And she will win. And Otto will be proud for her, of her. He will nod—and smile—in approval of the judgment.

Sarah and Otto sit in the kitchen, at that table full of odds and ends that can no longer be put away, of scraps of paper and grocery lists and forgotten telephone numbers. Sharps and flats and naturals. Thin chords. Melodies, and pieces of melodies all but forgotten. Stray bits of long lives.

Another day, worn through to another afternoon.

Is it cold out? There's not any wind. Everything out there is still. Just still. And quiet, in the afternoon.

And in the quiet of that afternoon, in all the stillness, the pianos in the music room open.

Four hands. A piece Sarah memorised when she was nine, in Sioux City. Somewhere in all those boxes of music there is a score that has a date written on it, in pencil: "Sarah memorised, 12 October 1917."

Otto looks up from the paper he has been puzzling at, and nods at Sarah. She straightens her shoulders, and poises her short, stubby fingers on the edge of the table. She closes her eyes, he closes his.

And then the pianos start to play. Four hands. And if ever the piece ends, if this music ever stops, all civilisation will applaud.

THE BORRONE BAND

Grandad played in a band as a young man. He told stories about playing on a big paddle-wheel steamer that ran from Memphis to New Orleans and back. They weren't showy stories, and you didn't learn much about the band or about riverboats from them. But they usually ended in a show. Somehow Grandad would just happen to have a broom in his hand—in the front parlor, or the living room—or maybe there would be a mop inexplicably leaning up against the back side of one of the columns that separated the parlor from the living room. And he would play "Rocked in the Cradle of the Deep" with the broom, creating a bass fiddle by licking the side of his index finger, laying it on the edge of the big polished mahogany cabinet the radio was in, and rubbing the broom across it like a bow.

I didn't know how he made the notes so clear and true. But he did. Later, when the Borrones got a big console Victrola to replace the old radio—it was a floor-model radio, in a cabinet as big as a full-sized dresser—he played on that.

Maybe, I thought, the box had to be some kind of music box to make all those notes.

Sometimes the inexplicable mop would have a string attached to the base of its handle, and Grandad would run that up through the eye in the top of the handle, and use the radio cabinet—or the Victrola—for resonance. He would tie the string through the eye of the handle, tight, and wedge the other up against the base of the cabinet. And he would pluck out "Three Blind Mice."

The stringed bass wasn't as good as the index-finger one he bowed with the broom handle. It had a thumpy sound, and wasn't really like music at all. Like saws that people play—to prove beyond doubt that God never meant for steel to sing!

But what Grandad bowed with the broomstick was music.

Of course he didn't play the broomstick—or the mop—in the riverboat band. He played a horn. Once when he and I were filling a big new storage closet on the inside back porch—an "overflower," he called it—we found an old silver B-flat cornet. We were moving stuff in boxes from the back of his and Gran's big closet in their bedroom out onto the porch. We opened all the boxes. Sometimes we threw the boxes away, but we kept what was in them. Grandad didn't volunteer to play the cornet, and it looked so old and battered that I didn't bother to ask him to. It didn't even seem worth my asking if I could have it. We just threw it up on top in the new closet, with some other stray things: old bedspreads and mothy blankets, and purses and crushed hats of Gran's.

"Toques," Grandad called them: Gran's old toques that Wilhelmina Howard made at her ladies' haberdashery, just off the far side of the square in Bowling Green.

Sometimes Grandad would fish down one of those fancy hats—they all had velvet roses across the front, and veils with big black lace dots on them, like spiders, or moles that hung out in front of your face. And he would model the hat while he made a game of serving drinks before Sunday dinner. Or he would put one on and come sweep the front porch to interrupt an otherwise quiet summer Sunday afternoon.

But he did play that cornet, when he was young.

About ten years after Grandad died we found a picture of him in the riverboat band. There were seven older men in summer suits and high, stiff collars—and Grandad. The biggest man played the bass, and two men with elaborate moustaches played banjos. A tall man with mutton-chop whiskers had a flute, and a skinny sad-eyed man held a long skinny clarinet straight up and down in front of him. A fat man with a trombone was sitting on a stool, next to another fat man with a little cornet, sitting on another stool. Grandad didn't have a cornet; he was the drummer. He had on a suit, too, but he was a young fellow, and he looked—to me—like I looked when I was eighteen or nineteen.

Then after Gran's death, when Dorothe and Jay were finally closing down the house—before it closed itself down, or fell down, since nobody had done anything for or to it in forty years—we found another picture, or set of pictures. Mom and Dorothe and I found it behind a cabinet in the dining room.

There were fifteen people in this band: fifteen separate photogaphs, arranged on a large grey mat-board. They all had on tight-fitting suits with lots of buttons, and wore little hats something like the ones train conductors wore. Some of them were older men, and Grandad was maybe twenty-five. He was the first one, on the top left. And he had a cornet in his hand.

My sister and I gave the picture to the Kentucky Historical Museum at the university. When we delivered it, the curator told us how delighted she was to have another picture of the Borrone Band.

"Borrone Band?" we asked.

"Oh, yes. We have another one out in the display cases. But it's not as good as this one."

"We have never heard it called the Borrone Band," my sister said.

The other picture was a group photo of eight men in shirt sleeves and straw hats. None of them were the men from the board we had just given to the museum—and no Grandad. But one of them was maybe Grandpa Borrone, Mom said later, when we got home. Grandpa when he was a younger man: before he was anybody's Grandpa, back when Grandad was a boy.

But we had never heard about that band. And anyway, Grandpa Borrone was a small, very Italian looking man with a big moustache—and there was no such person in the museum's Borrone Band.

The curator was sure, however. That's what the museum called it, and it was in their catalogue as such. It was registered, as history.

So that other Borrone Band is there, along with Grandad's, and as real and true or whatever as history is. But there's not a Borrone in it, and it doesn't belong to Borrone history. And nobody knows how it got there.

What goes on in people's minds? Why do they keep what they keep, tell what they tell, hide what they hide? Or make things up?

I never heard Grandad sing a note—except when he croaked "Three Blind Mice" to accompany his stringed mop-handle. Nobody would have thought of him as musical. Gran taught me songs, and Mom and Dorothe and Jay all sang. Billie sang her one song, "Mexicali Rose," over and over again. But Grandad didn't sing at all.

He didn't even sing in church. When we sall sang "Holy God We Praise Thy Name" at the end of benediction, Grandad would rock back and forth to the music, but he wouldn't sing. Didn't—though there was certainly music in him.

Why didn't Grandad tell us about the Borrone Band—about his, or about that other one? Maybe because it was called the Borrone Band. Grandad didn't have a very big tolerance for first-person pronouns or any other kind of self-advertisement. He probably wouldn't have liked having something named after him.

But his band, at any rate, had existed, and presumably—since each one of those men was pictured with his instrument—they made music. And the riverboat band must have made music, too. The music was what was important. And maybe the older band was called the Borrone Band because his father had organised it, to entertain at dances or at public functions like the town's Fourth of July picnics. And then Grandad himself, fifteen or twenty years later, put together another band, an almost official band, with uniforms. But neither Grandad nor his father ever called the band the Borrone Band.

MY MOTHER'S PIANO

We gave Mom a piano for Christmas. The first thing she did when she saw it was fall through the piano bench.

It was the Christmas of 1964. I went to the Baldwin factory in Cincinnati that September to pick it out. It was a walnut spinet. Ted and Ann and I gave it to her.

Mom had grown up playing the piano. It wasn't till she and Dad got married that she was ever without one. Her mother had a piano, though, a parlor grand Steinway that Grandad had bought when Mom was a little girl. I suspect the reason Mom and I always stopped by Gran's on the way home from school when I was little was the piano. Mom always played—or doodled, anyway—while she visited with Gran and Dorothe.

I thought that piano was the greatest thing in the world. Gran and Grandad had their record-player, but even though I knew how to play it, it wasn't anything like the piano. Even when I made it play "The Little Red Fox" backwards—and sang along with it—it wasn't as wonderful as the piano.

I didn't know how you learned to play the piano. I tried to teach myself to play like my mother playd, but it never sounded very good, and my fingers always got tangled up. And I couldn't figure out how you were supposed to know which keys made which noises before you struck them.

One afternoon Mom showed me middle C, and after that I started learning one-fingered versions of songs. My favorites were the May hymns: "Bring Flowers of the Fairest," "Tis the Month of Our Mother," and "O Mary We Crown Thee." I knew that Mom's first name was Mary, though everybody called her Elizabeth. And I played and sang those hymns for her.

I don't know what gave me the idea, but I decided we should give Mom a piano, and persuaded Ted and Annie to go in with me on it. Ted and I had both started our first real teaching jobs that year; Ann was a sophomore in college.

We were all home for Christmas. The Baldwin man was supposed to call our house when he got to Bowling Green. We were expecting him on the morning of ther twenty-second: my birthday. He called just after one o'clock.

Dad answered the phone in the den, and called me. I wanted to surprise him, too—I don't know why—so I went over to the other side of the house to take the call.

Of course Dad didn't hang up. I guess I knew he wouldn't: he was always an eavesdropper. The Baldwin man and I talked very circumspectly. I cut him off before he could mention a piano, and he caught on. He said he would be there in twenty minutes to see me, on his way to Nashville.

We had everything arranged. As soon as I got off the phone Ted grabbed Mom's coat and told her they had to go shopping. He needed to buy a present for somebody. She was busy in the kitchen, and didn't want to go.

"You're a big boy," she told Ted. "You can go shopping by yourself."

We buttoned her up, though, and pushed her out the door, protesting.

"You're being as nutty as fruitcakes," she said.

Dad was curious, but we didn't even have time to fight over his snooping, let alone answer his questions. Ann and Trish—Ted's wife—and I readjusted the furniture in the living room, and made a space on the far wall, under the big mirror.

The man arrived, and he and I trucked the piano in and uncovered it. I signed for the delivery and we got him out and gone. Ann took the sheet music she had hidden in her closet, and put it in the piano bench. We had "Paper Doll" and "Daddy's Little Girl," and *Oklahoma!* And *The Sound of Music.* I don't know why we had the two musicals. And "Galway Bay," and "You Can't Buy Your Way into Heaven."

When Ted brought Mom back she was still complaining. They hadn't Christmas shopped at all. When they got downtown, Ted had said they would never find a parking place on the Square and the stores would all be crowded, so they just came home.

"That's the dumbest trip I ever made in my life," Mom announced as they came in. "I don't know why I have to have smart kids, if they are as dumb as this!"

We all stood out of the way. She would take her coat over to her bedroom to hang it up.

She walked through the dining room and straight across the living room into her bedroom. When she came back out we were still standing there, watching.

"What in the world are you all doing?" she said.

And then she noticed it.

Mom plopped down on the bench, and put out her hands. After a few frozen seconds she said,

"I can't remember a thing. I can't remember a single God's blessed thing!"

Ann made her stand up, and opened the piano bench, and got out the music. Before she could close the top of the bench, though, Mom sat back down—and sat right through the bottom of it.

We pulled her out, and closed it. We didn't even notice that the bottom was broken—split right in two—till after the first long session was over, and things were returning to something as near to normal as our house ever was.

Once Mom started playing, she didn't need any music. She just sat there and played. I had never seen her—never saw her—so happy.

Gran's piano hadn't been tuned, then, in twenty years. Nobody ever touched it any more—hadn't, for years. Not even me. Once when I was in college Phil Hurley had come to visit, and when we went in to Gran's he ran over to the piano and started to play the one Rachmaninoff that he knew half of. It was so hideous sounding that he stopped even before he ususlly did.

Mom hadn't played since Ann was born. But she hadn't forgotten anything, and played—to our ears—like a concert pianist.

I have no idea what the rest of that day was like. Maybe we even forgot that it was my birthday. Mom was happy, and for the first time in our lives, *our* house was full of music.

Everybody always sang, of course. Mom sang all the time. "Paper Doll," and "Galway Bay"—Gran's song, and mine, but Mom sang it too. And "When You are in Love."

When I was a kid in high school, Mom sang all the popular songs kids listened to—'fifties songs—but either she was making jokes or she just wasn't very careful about the words.

You're walking behind me
On my wedding day,
And I'll hear you promise
That you'll go away.

When three other kids and I formed a quartet—I was the bass, at thirteen—Mom taught us songs like "Five Foot Two" and "Bye Bye Blues." Dorothe taught us "The Sweetheart of Sigma Chi." Bob Dance got sheet music marked with ukeleli chords, and learned to play them, but none of us could read music so somebody had to teach us the melodies.

Eventually Mom got tired of hearing us squawk in adolescent unison, and made Ted start teaching us about harmony.

Of course Ted sang. He had a good voice. When I was in high school he taught me barbershop, taught me to love those sweet, close harmonies. And sang them with me. The two of us could make a pretty good barbershop quartet. Ted sang top tenor and baritone, I sang melody and bass.

Annie sang, too. She was a little girl—seven, maybe, or eight—when she sang "It Takes Two to Tangle," after Teresa Brewer. And even though Dad couldn't carry a tune, he whistled when he painted the house or snapped beans or shucked corn.

But we had never had real music in our house till Mom's piano came.

ANTONIO BORRONE SPEAKS OF PERGOLESI AND MOZART

Buona sera. Let me introduce myself. I say that because I have been lost—or all but lost—in history for many, many years, and no one remembers me. I am Antonio Borroni, composer, who lived a very long life.

That I was a composer is what has been lost, because none of my music survives. The encyclopaediae of music record that I lived, and that I composed music—but no one has heard my music in more than two hundred years. I might as well have been an ancient Etruscan.

But it is not because of my music that I intrude upon you. My authority is not the music that I wrote—it may not, in fact, have been very good—but the music that I heard. And in my lifetime—it was a long life, justified more by what I was priviliged to hear than by my own accomplishments—I heard much music: much great music.

What I heard inspired me. And though I had not the talent to respond appropriately to that inspiration as a composer, I was inspired. And I knew—better, I suppose, than most of my contemporaries—just how great that music was. I knew its greatness well enough to know that my own music was inferior.

I was born in Bologna, not in Roma as the music historians would tell you. (Did they ever get anything right? They would flat a needle, or confuse *baroque* with barbecue.) And the year of my birth was 1724, not 1738. I was the only one of my parents' children to survive infancy. Both my mother and my father had musical ambitions for me, and I began my studies with the *maestro di capella* in Bologna. In 1734 my father moved us to Roma, in order that I might have a better musical education.

Not loing after our arrival in Roma, my father took me to hear Giovanni Battista Pergolesi's opera, *L'Olympiade.* I remember little of it, except the overture, which was loud and brassy and—to my young ears—very beautiful. My father loved the opera, and immediately set out to find Pergolesi and procure for me a place under his tutrelage. But Pergolesi was ill, and had already returned to his native Napoli.

The great music of the day was Pergolesi's, my father said, and Pergolesi was in Napoli. So we decamped for Napoli, and there I began my serious work as a student of music. But not with Pergolesi, for in March of 1836 the young genius died.

But I had heard *L'Olympiade,* and I knew that Pergolesi was the great musician of our time. I continued my studies in Napoli, and began first to compose and then to teach there. And Napoli was the place for a young musician to be, because as Pergolesi's posthumous fame spread—my father had judged his work rightly—Napoli became one of the most important centers for music in all of Europe.

Giovanni Battista Pergolesi—whose music I had heard, first in Roma and then in Napoli—was more important and popular after his death than he was in life. But fame is fickle, and by the end of the eighteenth century he was lost, forgotten. And now—two hundred years later—he has been found again. I have remained lost, however, even in Italy. And when, in the nineteenth century of this age of forgetting, one of my great-great-great-grandchildren left Italy and went to th United States of America, he and his young wife Louisa didn't take me with them. No. They took diamonds, not my music. And then they sold fruit in Kentucky.

One American Borroni, Umberto, played a horn on a riverboat on the Mississippi river, and later had a band in a small town in southern Kentucky.

I have seen a photograph of him: he was a young man who looked just like me. But except for Umberto, there was no Borroni music after me, and my music—whatever it was worth—is lost.

But I knew Pergolesi's music. And that is much more important than my music.

In my time, Giovanni Baptista Pergolesi was the *great* Pergolesi, the *inimitable* Pergolesi. For a while. And then the music changed—tastes changed—and nobody wanted to imitate Pergolesi, or even to hear the real and inimitable Pergolesi. And he was lost.

Not altogether lost. People have always listened to his *Stabat Mater,* and *La Serva Padrona,* his famous intermezzo, was a popular piece for many, many years. But otherwise he was forgotten. By 1800 his music had disappeared from the concert halls and the churches; his operas were forgotten.

At the heighth of his posthumous fame, however, in Napoli and in Roma, in Vienna and in Munich, in Paris and in London, everything had been Pergolesi. Literally. It was not enough to listen to his music, and talk about him, and acclaim him as the father—young as he was, or had been—of the "new music" of the eighteenth century. No. More than that. Everything was Pergolesi—even if it wasn't! Mountebanks of all crawls of life, musical pimps, opportunists, they sold music written by who knows who, claiming it was Pergolesi's. They made Pergolesi as prolific as Mozart would make Mozart, even without the extra ten years of life Mozart wsas given in this world.

There was ten times as much Pergolesi *not* by Pergolesi as there was by Pergolesi. And some of what was Pergolesi was plagiarised, of course, from Pergolesi.

In my time his most famous opera was *Adriano in Siria,* which he wtote in 1734 for King Carlos of Napoli. The next year he wrote *L'Olympiade*—the opera which I heard, as a small boy—for the *carnavale* in Roma. The Roman audience liked trumpets. So Pergolesi added a long trumpet fanfare from the beginning of the overture to *Adriano,* and several other brassy pleasures for his Roman audience, and called this piece the overture to *L'Olympiade.*

My great-great-great-great-grandson Umberto, who played the cornet in a band on the Mississippi River, might have inherited his love for the horn from my pleasure in hearing *L'Olympiade.* If so, that is my gift to the new world. But much better, surely, to have played a horn for Pergolesi than to play in a brass band on a riverboat!

Pergolesi lived a very short life: only twenty-six years. He wrote for six years. Of course he wrote when he was younger, when he was a student in Napoli. It was said that when he was only sixteen years old he improvised melodies on his violin that were so enchantingly beautiful that other students would stop their practice and listen in wonder. But the music that he wrote down—the music that was performed, first in Napoli and then in Roma, was all written between 1731 and 1736.

Pergolesi was only fourteen years older than I. But he was a genius, and already—before his twenty-third birthday—he had transformed opera.

His operas had not just form, but melody, and feeling. They democratised serious music.

Pergolesi was not simply a student of music, even as a boy. Students of music learn what is alrady known—and eventually they know so much of what is already know that they can't find room in their heads for anything else. Their knowledge prejudices them against the large, open full world of sound and passion and life.

True, there are only so many notes, and only so many permutations of the order in which those notes can be played or sung. But those so manys are so much reduced when one applies rules to how they may be used. And Pergolesi broke the rules.

The forms of music changed. He liberated music from the patterns that had been practiced by composers for a hundred years. Scarlatti was the court composer in Naples for forty years, and his one hundred operas were all written in the tradition of those hundred years: perfecting it, perhaps, but also reinforcing and repeating it. Pergolesi probably wasn't thinking revolutionary thoughts when he started to write music: he probably wasn't intending anything so grand or before his time as liberation. Such ambitions belonged to later generations. Pergolesi was just hearing in his head longer phrases of melody than the forms of his time allowed: and instead of trimming those melodies to fit the forms, he chose for the integrity of those melodies and abandoned the forms he had been taught.

Some of those musical phrases he took straight from the streets of Naples. That's the democracy he brought to music. Through some of the sounds of Pergolesi's music were strange to the ears of the inhabitants of the Neopolitan court, they were familiar to the people of that warm, vivid, melodious city.

Pergolesi's greatest music, however, was written not for the Neopolitan court, or for the people of the streets of Naples, nor for the opera stage there or in Roma. It was written for the church. I remember hearing his *Stabat Mater*—composed when he was dying, in 1736—for the first time. I was moved beyond tears by the eloquent, loving sadness of the *Cuius animam* and again by the *Fac me vere tecum flere,* and by the final *Quando corpus morietur.*

It was said that Pergolesi wrote his *Stabat Mater* to replace Scarlatti's. It did—and replaced, in my mind, every piece of church music I had ever heard. There had never been anything like this, except in the articulate hearts of lovers and maybe saints. The sweetness of the *Stabat Mater* was stolen by Pergolesi's genius straight from the soul of sorrowing love. For how many centuries had humans waited to hear the tenderest centers of their beings speak!

I knew, hearing this music, that I was closer to the world in which the Gods must live than I had ever dreamed possible. Pergolesi was like a young Prometheus, stealing fire from Kronos. But Pergolesi's gift was more than light, or intelligence: it was imagination itself, the dreams of the Gods out of which this world was made.

Pergolesi died when he was but twenty-six years old. What would he not have done had he lived? I, who lived a very long life, cringe guiltily when I think of how he would have lived my years, filling the world with his music.

I had no significant gift as a musician, and it is no great loss—no loss at all—that none of my music survives. But I was gifted: given a great gift with my long life. Nor did I hear Giovanni Battista Pergolesi, I heard Mozart.

Wolfgang Amadeus Mozart was born in 1756, just twenty years after Pergolesi's death. I was thirty-two then. Mozart was born in Salzburg; I was working and teaching in Naples. By the time he was seven or eight he was composing excellent work in the style of the time; I was writing operas, then—none of them very successful, none of them memorable—in Venezia, and then in Prague. When Mozart was thirteen, he began a tour of the Italian cities, performing his own music—and it was then that I first heard of the young genius from Salzburg.

The first time I actually heard his music was not until 1773. He was all of seventeen then. I heard his *Exsultate, Jubilate* in Milan, and then a few months later the Symphony in G Minor, in Salzburg. In 1775 I journeyed from Stuttgart to Salzburg to hear the *Missa Brevis* in G.

I had never forgotten Pergolesi. His *Stabat Mater* was as clear in my head and in my heart as my mother's face, or my own private idea of heaven. And it was ever-present in that part of my being which knew to breathe without being prompted to do so. Pergolesi's *Stabat Mater* was an intimate and necessary part of my life.

But Mozart—Mozart took me altogether *out of* my life.

Yet his music was not other-worldly. Though Mozart's violins, his right hand on the fortepiano, and the long *legati* his sopranos sang were the very ether of transcendence, they were clearly, palpably a mortal's creation. What made Mozart's music his—superbly his, inimitably his—was that it expressed so utterly and absolutely a human soul climbing out of its own limitations, but never for a moment surrendering itself to God.

If Pergolesi democratised music, brought the people into it and freed its form to match their form, Mozart freed us to live, if only for the duration of its miracle, within the larger possibility which it created. Had Mozart lived to my age, he might have created the music which would have inspired genius—not simply musical genius, but human genius, the genius that would recreate the human soul as the image of the beautiful, benevolent God.

When I was a young man I was in love with music. I wanted to be a musician, a composer. I composed—but when I heard Pergolesi I knew even before I had begun my career that I was not a composer. Hearing Pergolesi, I knew also that I loved music more than I had ever dreamed possible. Then, nearly half a century later, I heard Mozart. How could one life contain two such experiences? I was truly blessed—I am truly blessed.

And that my music has all disappeared, been forgotten and then lost, matters not. Why should men and women play or listen to Borroni, when God has given them life to play or hear Pergolesi's *Stabat Mater* and Mozart's *Coronation Mass* or the impossibly beautiful harmonies of the "Ave Verum"?

Listening to the "Agnus Dei" of the *Coronation Mass* or the "Ave Verum"—or any of the later piano or violin concertos—is like holding the wafer on your tongue as a child, and knowing then in your innocent faith that God is in your mouth, dissolving. Or it is like making love: but ten thousand times more brave and glorious. It is so wonderful, so beautiful, you would like it to last forever; but at he same time, *because* it is so exquisitely beautiful you want it to reach its climax—and then it is over.

And everything must be still. Utterly, absolutely still. No applause. No talking about it. No thinking. Not even any breathing. The world has gone to God, and you with it.

Were it not that I am in love with the great music which I heard in my lifetime, I would be dead. Were I not so inspired by that music, I would have died long ago, and left behind me but the few genes that have occasionally spurred my descendants toward music. Berti Borroni, a century or more after me, played a cornet. His grandsons sang, and one of them kneww and loved Pergolesi's *Stabat Mater*, and every note of Mozart's. He even sang in the chorus of *Cosi fan Tutti* once, and also in *Don Giovanni.*

I didn't hear *Cosi fan Tutti* or *Don Giovanni,* but I understand from the angels that they, too, are great works of genius. And genius blesses life.

LAST SONGS

It occurred to me when Billie died. She lived in Washington—had gone there in 1940 with Mary, her girlfriend, and they had stayed. But before that, the three of us used to go for drives in Bill's little Ford coupe. I was still small enough to ride stetched out up behind the seat, in the space in front of the rear window.

Billie would sing as she drove. "Mexicali Rose," over and over, drive after drive. Out the Louisville road, past the L&N underpass. Out the Nashville road as far as Lost River. Down the Russellville road to Mrs. Higginsbottom's farm, or maybe all the way to South Union. Out the Scottsville road to the haunted house on the hill before Middle Bridge. Way out the Cemetery road and off through Mr. Howell's farm to the bluff in front of Aunt Rose's, Billie singing as we drove.

Mexicali Rose, I love you.
I'll come back to you some sunny day . . .

That's the only song I ever heard her sing, I think.

Billie was the first of her generation to die. She hadn't been home for twenty years—four months short of twenty years, to be exact. Mary and Dorothe had a fight at Gran's funeral, and Billie and Mary never came back to Bowling Green again. They left that afternoon by taxi for Nashville, sixty-four miles away, and flew back to Washington. And dared anybody to come to visit them. I went once, and a few years later my brother went. And then one year I was in Washington just after Christmas, and telephoned to ask if I could come out.

"No," Bill said. "Don't bother."

Bill didn't have a funeral. Mary had her cremated, and buried her ashes in the little plot she and Mary had bought in Arlington. Mary called Dorothe to tell her, and then she left to visit her widowed sister-in-law in London. Nobody ever heard from her again.

Mom and Dad forgot to tell us about her death. It fell out casually a few weeks later when my sister and her family were at home for a visit. Ann was talking with Mom in the kitchen.

"Billie died," Mom said.

"When?"

"Oh, two weeks ago. Mary called and told Dorothe."

Ann phoned me. "As of two weeks ago," she said, "there isn't a Billie."

That's when it occurred to me. The first thing I thought of—no, before I thought, while I was starting to think, to line up all the Billie memories and sort through them, go through the usual procedure of filtering out what to keep, like pictures that you will closet away in the album of your mind.

What came up first in my head was "Mexicali Rose." It was probably running in my head before I noticed it there, because when I noticed it I had already found—without trying, without thinking—all the words.

Mexicali Rose, I love you.
I'll come back to zou some sunny day.
Always I'll be dreaming of you,
Every hour that I'm gone away.
Dry your big brown eyes and smile, dear,
Banish all your cares and please don't cry.
Kiss me once again and hold me—
Mexicali Rose, good-bye.

When I discovered myself singing it, in my head, I stopped thinking and just said it: out loud, to Ann.

I could remember Bill singing it, and us singing it together. I was four, maybe. Bill's voice was very deep. She had a big, rich baritone voice. But that's the only song I ever heard her sing.

And when Ann and I finished talking that day, I sang "Mexicali Rose" all the way through for Billie, remembering us. And then I sang it again, just for her. As a sort of formal good-bye. No more Bill. No more Billie. *Marian Beatrice Borrone, good-bye.*

And then I thought, I should have sung "Galway Bay" for Gran. At her funeral. Or maybe after, at her grave.

When I was little, every Sunday my mother would sit down at the big old piano in the formal living room at Gran's house, and I would stand behind Mom. The rest of the family—the Borrones and the Hornbacks—would be over in the parlor, beyond the big wooden columns that separated the two rooms.

My mother would play, and I would sing "Galway Bay" for Gran.

If you ever go across the sea to Ireland,
Then maybe at the closing of your day
You will sit and watch the moon rise over Claddagh,
And see the sun go down o'er Galway Bay.

An immigrant's song—or an immigrant's son's song—written in the thirties. New then, I guess. Bing Crosby and I sang it. And Gran loved it, though she didn't have any idea where Galway Bay was in Ireland, or where her family—Monaghans—had come from, across those seas.

Just to hear again the ripple of the trout stream,
The women in the meadows making hay,
And to sit beside a turf fire in your cabin
And see the barefoot gosoons at their play.

Oh the breezes blown across the seas from Ireland
Are perfumed by the heather as they go,
And the women in the uplands digging praties
Speak a language that the strangers do not know.

It always made Gran cry. She loved sad songs. She taught me "She's only a bird in a gilded cage," and "My darling Nelly Gray, they have taken you away." And "There's a long, long trail a-winding into the land of my dreams." We would cry together, when I was little, when we sang them.

And if there's going to be a life hereafter,
And faith, I know for sure there's going to be,
I will ask my God to let me make my heaven
In that dear land across the Irish sea.

I used to wonder whether Gran would go to heaven or to Ireland when she died. I asked her once. She just laughed. She wasn't going to either one of them in any hurry, she said—even though she had made her will.

Gran and I had pinned little pieces of paper to the bottoms of all the chairs in the house, and stuck them to the bottoms of tables and up under all the beds, telling who got what when she died. We changed them, every so often. After I grew up, Ann was around to help her make her revisions.

When Gran died, in 1970, I don't remember anybody looking for her will. Everybody knew about it, of course—I always told Mom when Gran and I changed bequests. But there wasn't any bequeathing to do, really, by the time Gran died. And went to Ireland.

I knew what I would sing for Jay, Mom's brother. He wrote a poem, once, years ago, before he had the accidental lobotomy that saved his life but took his mind. Mom set it to music for him.

> *I wish I could fashion a locket of sun,*
> *And a necklace of stars when the night has begun.*
> *I wish I could bathe in the dew of a rose,*
> *And carpet my home with the wild moss that grows.*
> *I wish I could weave frosted cobwebs together*
> *And use them for curtains in cold winter weather.*
> *How fleeting these beauties I look on enchanted,*
> *And wonder if all the world takes them for granted.*

For the last twenty-five years of his life Jay had no memory. He could make sense of things, but he would lose that sense as soon as he had understood it. Once he realised what had happened to him, he quit trying to carry on real conversations, and told jokes instead—which he read off slips of paper he carried around in his shirt pocket. Jay couldn't even tell family stories—he couldn't get them right. But every now and then he would recite his poem.

In 1990 we all went home for Mom and Dad's sixtieth wedding anniversary. Ann and Guy and their son Cameron came from Pensacola, and I drove down from Ann Arbor. Ted sent his three sons from California.

When Jay met young Teddy's wife, he recited his poem for her.

"I wrote that," he told her. "That's everything I know."

I intended to sing his song for him before he died—just mention it, maybe, on one of my Thusday afternoon visits. "Do you still remember your poem, Jay? The one Mom wrote the music for?" But I didn't. After

Dorothe called to tell me that he had died I sang it, though—to remember him by, or with.

It's not that I am any great singer, though I like to sing. Ted was the one with the good voice. Singing makes *sense* to me. So I sing a lot.

I didn't know what to sing for Dot. Some funny song: she would want that.

"It doesn't hurt when I fall down these days," she told me once. "I've shrunk so much it's only a foot or two to the ground." Or talking about dying: "You can just push me over the fence into the cemetery. I'll know the way to our house from there."

Maybe, I thought, I should sing "Doin' What Comes Naturally" for her. She had taught that to me before I was old enough to know what it meant. It was one of her Dorothy Shay songs that Gran wouldn't listen to.

I knew what I would sing for Mom. She was already sixty-four when Gran died. Mom died at ninety-three. Toward the end her eyes weren't as bright as they used to be, but they still smiled when she was happy. And when I went to see her every afternoon she was happy. And when we kissed, and kissed some more, she would laugh. "We are something else!" she would say. She grew frail, and her memory faded, and sometimes—when she was tired—she didn't make sense. But even then her eyes would smile at me, and she would lay her head on my chest and let me hold her.

"I think," she would say, "that we kind of like each other."

And no matter how she felt, or even if she was angry at her situation, her life"I never thought it would come to this!" she would say, or "I just want to get out of here"—even then, she could stop, check herself, and tell me:

"Now don't you go wasting your time sitting here with me. You have a life to live. You go do what you ought to be doing. I'll be happy just knowing you're doing it."

Mom had the finest mind I ever knew. The finest understanding of life, too. And when Ted and Ann and I hal talked about them growing old—Mom and Dad, and Mom's sisters and her brother—we had always said, "Well, we can depend on Mom."

She designed the house we built. And she taught me to design houses, and how to fix most everything. She taught me to tell stories, too, and to sing. She taught Ted to draw, and taught Ann to paint. She made all of our clothes, when we were young—and made all of her own clothes, all her life.

I remember how excited I was to start school. But school wasn't nearly as much fun—or as exciting, or as educational—as home. So three or four days a week I stayed home with Mom. In third grade we overdid it, and when I got home with my report card at the end of the year Mom had to call the nuns.

"Do you want him in third grade again next year?" She asked.

After that I was free—didn't *have* to go to school. I usually just stayed at home, and let Mom teach me.

I knew what to sing for Mom. And I knew I shouldn't wait. I should sing it while she could still hear it, and understand it. And I did sing it, almost every day; for four years.

You can't buy the sunshine at twilight,
You can't buy the moonlight at dawn.
You can't buy your youth when you're growing old,
Or your life when your heartbeat's still.

You can't buy your way into heaven,
Though you may possess wealth untold,
And just like your mother you'll ne'er find another
Though you have all the world and its gold.

And Dad. Dad didn't sing. He wasn't at all musical. When Ted and I were little he would do "I know a place where the birds sing bass." He must have known enough of a tune for us to learn it, because I still know it. But that was his only song.

Mom used to sing "Daddy's Little Girl" for him, after Ann was born. Then, when we gave her the piano, she could play it for him—but Ann was nineteen then. One night—I was visiting them—Mom was sitting at the piano after dinner, doodling. Dad was half-napping in his chair. I was standing behind Mom.

"Sing something," she said, looking at me in the mirror.

I suggested "Daddy's Little Girl."

She doodled on a bit before she said anything. Then she shook her head.

"I can't play that any more. It makes him cry."

I understood: sure. When I used to sing it for Dad—practicing—I would cry, too.

Annie is nearly seventy now.

I sang "Way Down Home" for Ted when he died. He taught me that, back when we used to sing barbershop harmonies together, the two of us singing all four parts.

Way down home,
Among the fields of cotton,
Way down home,
That's where I long to be.
Way down home,
Where memory's forgotten.
My mind is free
And I long to be
Way down home.
Way down home.

When Ted's youngest son Bob called to tell me he had died—of a stroke—I sang that as soon as we had hung up.

And when I go? I want to sing just before it's all over. Not out of vanity. Not for the sake of some last silly self-assertion, either. I just want to sing. I have no idea what, yet. Maybe one last bit of harmony, with the world. Maybe all the notes at once.

THE WASHINGTON POST MARCH

The Washington Post March. Oh, I remember. In the Western Gym in Bowling Green. The Louisville sports-writers always called it a "band-box" or "the big red barn."

It is halftime. The band sits in the balcony, on the south end. Everybody else in the balcony just sits on the big two-foot-wide platform steps, but the band has folding metal chairs. And they play the Washington Post March. *Da-dum-da-dah, da-dum-da-dah, da-da-dum-dah.*

As I remember it my childhood turns into an eternity of the Washington Post March. I am always there, in the Gym, sitting with all the other kids on the floor of the wooden track around the inner lip of the balcony, with my legs dangling down over the bleachers below. I look down at the people walking back and forth at the edge of the basketball court, nodding hellos, carrying cokes and popcorn. Two small boys dressed in red warm-up suits trot up and down the floor with push-mops. Off in the distance, across and down in the far corner of the balcony, the band plays the Washington Post March. And everybody seems to be moving in time with it. We all seem to be there in time with its elegant and practised serenity. *Da-dum-da-dah, da-dum-da-dah.*

What music! The world is in focus at hip-joiints and on the balls of feet. It asks for public, universal ballet. The big red barn becomes a dance-hall.

No. Nobody is dancing. See—they are just walking. Nobody is even keeping time to the music. They are all relaxing. And since the band always plays the Washington Post March now, just at the start of halftime, just as soon as the teams get off the floor and the mop-boys come out: since it's always the Washington Post March now, nobody pays any attention.

My mother walks by below, and smiles up at me. I can't quite make out how old she is. I am ten or twelve or fourteen so she is forty. Younger than I am. Much younger. But she looks like my mother, always. It is the Washington Port March that makes her look that way forever. In the easy rhythm of *da-dum-da-dah, da-dum-da-dah,* she walks by me again and again, looks up and smiles at her son. *Da-dum-da-dah, da-dum-da-dah.*

The feeling is sweet. Halftime is forever. The band in its red and grey uniforms keeps playing the Washington Post March, generation after generation. Its calm repetetiions are all ther assurance I need that this time is eternity. I am smiling. There is no need to talk. Shoulder to shoulder, elbow into elbow, thigh to thigh crowded around the edge and leaning against the rail with my friends, I am happy. The whole world is preserved. The floor shines. My father is the coach; he is still a young man. Grandad sits erect in his bleacher seat just beneath and behind me. My mother keeps walking by and smiling up at me. *Da-dum-da-dah, da-dum-da-dah.* The game will never resume, never end. It is halftime forever now.

And as I write this I move my head ever so slightly to the rhythm of that tune that never ends. I keep time with it, carefully, easily, the inside of my head moving back and forth so very slightly to its rhythm.

Yes. I keep time with it: keep it—the whole world, forever—in the Western Gym, the band-box, the big red barn.

Da-dum-da-dah

MR. LEOPOLD BLOOM DETERMINES (TENTATIVELY) TO LEARN THE BLOWBAGS

But Molly?

And not those maggotty things at Lionel Marks's. A good set—do you call them it set thing instrument. Anyway it will cost.

No. No way. Mistake even to ask. Still, free ad in the programme—Mr. Bloom's instrument from Lionel Marks's no Piggott's—over time would pay. Ten—say twenty—concerts a year.

And practice. I wonder do they wear out. Like trousers. Blowbags too in a way. How many years a good pair?

And lessons. That, too. Them. How to? Some way, there's always a will there's a. Perhaps natural genius. Never tell.

The artist always finds a way. A touch of the masterstroke. Prodigy. Prodigal. Prodigious.

Sacrifice. But what? Kidneys? Lemon soap. Gift for Martha. The holy sacrifice of the dringadring.

But blowbags? The pipes, traditional instrument.

And of his ass he made a horn, with his tooraloom tooraloom tay. Tied to a tooraloom tooraloom tay. Yes.

Do his duty. For Ireland home and beauty. The dedicated artist. Bloobloo. Dloodloo.

That honking thing—the drone they call it—as a cover. Wrong notes don't seem so wrong, covered with that. Kran. Krandle. Let my epitaph be.

A patriotic thing. Compose perhaps a national anthem. Let my epitaph. Nations of the world. I'll do it.

But Molly?

Not exactly accompaniment. Complement. Mrs. L. M. Bloom, soprano, with Mr. L. M. Bloom, blowbags. Bagpipes.

Won't bag many a tour with that. Advertise better. The celebrated Irish soprano, Mrs. Marian de la Flower á Voglio, accomapanied (from the rere) by Don Poldo O'Virago, the world-renowned innovator of the Irish horn.

The scapegoat's bladder.

Winds from the south. Upside down. Same shape they are. Yes. Tongueing it them they say.

What would happen if you blew in it? Give her gas.

Keep her on key. Me the drone, she the melody. Me air in, she air out.

In one end and out the other. No, ear. Still. It works both ways.

A great organ.

Love's old sweet seated one day on the. Mollody.

But how to pay for the lessons?

It's all practice, of course. Perhaps a book. Books are the best teachers, or experience.

Mouthpiece. Take it home, learn to tongue it properly. The notes. Dear Henry. My patients.

Could practice on those statues. Inserting the catheter. Dr. Bloom, in the course of his experiments in callipygnics.

Do you even use your tongue? Or just blow. O. And the elbow. Funny the rhyme. To make the no the do. Do re me. Do re mi fa sol. No me fa. My fa. Mi fa sol.

Birthright. Music a sort of birthright.

Easier if I could sing.

Fa sol sol fa.

Sofie.

Martha.

Can't sing. Swurls. Churls. Those lovely seaside.

Those lovely.

The lovely, haunting air. The piper sits on the beach in the gathering dusk, playing by himself with himself *al mano.* She hears it, lovely, haunting. Air.

Drone.

Piping pwee my little pwee.

And shee. Pwee. She. Me.

Singing *la ci darem al mano* yes together hand in hand. Molly bowing, thank you thank you. Flowers for Mrs. Flower. Sweets to the. Blooms for Mrs. Bloom.

I drone. And she *voglio.* Poglio and Moglio. Poglio *voglio* Moglio. Sweets for the sin.

The Right Honourable Marian McTweedy, in concert with (accompanied by) (together with) (in union with) the Bloom the Oneal, kneeling Oneal on the Rock of Cashel upside down and bottoms up bagpiper impossible

A decent descant, hers and mine.

Tomorrow?

Surprise her. Wait till. Upstairs, practicing. The queen. And I in the kitchen, eating bread and kidney. Then the secret note, finding the pitch her pitch under the pillow. Yes. Then her, letting it out, stronger.

Accompanying. Her. Me. The alto. The Irish oboe. Ebony obone. Yes.

And she, hearing it.

Poldy? Is that the cat? It the kettle boiling?

No. Whistling. Swurls.

My kidney simply swurls.

No.

The lovely sound. You are my flower of the mountain

And the sun shines the wind blows for you

By yon bonnie brae.

And by yon bonnie breeze.

Bunny breeze.

Bunny prints. Bunny prince sailing, over the sea to Skye. Tralala. Tralala.

Practice makes perfect. Those statues. Perfect example of the art of the Greeks.

The arse of the Greeks.

The grease, too. Ham and ham. We'll go.

La ci darem la ham an ham.

Homonym. It's the rhyme. Her note and mine. Yes.

We are a nation. We live together.

The new national music. In concert. The bottom and the top. Tip-top. Complete. Together. Smelling her.

Yes.
Would you be smelling her?
O, I would.
O, I would be.
O, I would be smelling.
Her. Her O.
Utterly arsely Irish.
The whole. The music's whole. Complete. Concert.
Content.

Are you happy in that other world? I do not like that other world. Swurled.

And he?

Let him sing with M'Coy's wife.

Getting it up.

She playing with him.

Yes.

Still . . .

Avis rara. Rare bird. My rare bird. Rere bird, too.

Yes.

La ci darem la mano. Hand in hand. And man to man. Or woman.

But not just any. Rere regardant, the artist's eye.

Who is Dexter Optic, I wonder.

Arsenic. That's a word for her.

There is a blessing in this gentle—that's Yeats, I think—in this gentle breeze. For this gentle breeze relief much thanks, she said. Muchibus thankibus, Hamlet. And O. And O.

O.

Should I?

Not the bur. Must be the

Yes.

It must be the

Yes. I will. We will, in concert. The sound of music.

Just a song at

And I kiss your bottom, my blossom bottom from the south bottom kissing your eyes with the touch of a poet

Kidneys beyond recall

Yes.

No gas. And not just the bur, either.
Not just the drone to the tuning fork turning, turning
to say
Yes.
But yes.
And O, he made himself a horn of his ass her bottom
and he said yes he said yes there is a blessing in this gentle
The music of the spheres. The true Irish air. Yes.
Kyrie! Kyrie! Kyrie Eleison!

OH, TO BE A 'CELLO

Some years ago now—it was in 1971, to be precise, on a beautiful autumn afternoon, on the King's Road in London—I was walking past the Chelsea Town Hall, enjoying life and enjoying my life, and singing. I was singing an old Irish hymn, "Morning Has Broken," popularised just that year by a man who called himself Cat Stevens.

Morning has broken like the first morning,
Blackbird has spoken like the first bird . . . .

All of a sudden, a wee small older lady stopped, dead still, in front of me.

I walk fast, even when I'm just strolling along enjoying life and singing a sweet song. If I hadn't also been looking at where I was going—looking right at that little lady when she stopped—I would have run over her.

She just stopped, dead still, and turned around. "Well, if you aren't the canary!" she said.

I'm nobody's canary. But I do love music—and I try to sing. All the time, or almost all the time.

When a group of my University of Michigan colleagues and I founded the Society of Bremen Scholars, in honor of the Musicians of Bremen and in protest against the misdirection of our university, I was assigned the part of the donkey, who was a baritone. I'm not a canary, by any stretch of anybody's imagination. If you want to call me something—besides agitator, teacher, pest, and fool—you should probably call me a baritone. I'm a baritone, however, who has spent his whole long life longing to be a tenor—or to sing bass.

But over time, I have become a bit more comfortable with who I am, and what I am. And Yo-Yo Ma was partly responsible for my mellowing: him and his 'cello.

The 'cello is a baritone instrument. It and I sing in the same range. And my bias for the 'cello is thus in part personal—embarrassingly chauvinistic and egotistical, you might say, if you wanted to be hard on me.

But I do love the 'cello. And I want to try to explain to you why I love it and its lovely, movingly lovable music.

Sometimes I envy tenors, or sopranos. I envy them for *where* they sing, up there beyond the world of vocal chords and lungs and breath. To want to reach a note that's out of your range is like swimming up to the surface in a pool—and finding a glass lid between you and the air.

I can *think* those high, clear notes—but I know I can never make them, realise them, sing them.

I love violins—but I don't think I have ever *envied* a violin its voice. Maybe I only envy other people—not instruments.

Come to think of it, I don't *really* envy tenors and sopranos when I hear them: I love to hear them, open my heart to them with gratitude and wonder. I only feel envy when I'm trying to sing, and bump into my limits.

> *Morning has broken like the first morning,*
> *Blackbird has spoken, like the first bird.*
> *Praise for the singing, praise for the morning,*
> *Praise for their springing fresh from the world.*

I am sure I wasn't much of a canary for that lady in London. I blush at the thought of what I really sounded like. She could have been run over by a crow!

I remember the first time I went to hear an opera. It was *Aida.* The NBC Opera Company—back in the days when radio networks had orchestras and even opera companies!—was performing *Aida* for the inauguration of O'Laughlin Auditorium at St. Mary's College in Indiana. I was a sophomore at Notre Dame University at the time, and my roommates and I went across the road to see and hear it. After the performance—because Jack Moynahan's older sister was somebody important at St. Mary's—we got to go backstage. Skip Johnson met one of the tenors.

"I love *Aida,*" Skip told the man. "I go around all the time singing the grand march." The tenor smirked at him, professionally. "You must be quite a trumpet," he said.

Flashy people, flashy music, flashy wit. Spectacle, elephants, crowds. But give me the 'cello any day—even if it doesn't have those highest notes, and seems sometimes, at the top of its range, to be straining toward but not quite reaching impossible heaven.

Walt Whitman, in his *Song of Myself,* writes: "I hear the violincello—'tis the young man's heart's complaint." I like that—though it seems to me that the 'cello is more middle-aged than young.

John Townsend Trowbridge agrees:

With years a richer life begins,
The spirit mellows:
Ripe age gives tone to violins,
Wine, and good fellows.

Or at least he should agree. *'Cellos* makes just as good a rhyme for *mellows* as *fellows* does—and the 'cello is the mellowest instrument of them all.

With years our richer lives begin,
The spirt mellows:
Ripe age gives tone to wine and men,
Like eloquent 'cellos.

Isn't that better? And who was John Townsend Trowbridge, anyway?

Maybe someone—maybe even me—should write a little book about the 'cello in literature. Or in art and literature. There must be—indeed are—some great paintings of people with 'cellos.

There's that one of the dog musicians: it's a companion to the one of the dogs playing poker. In the music painting the collie is playing the 'cello, I think. And Watteau, that painter famous for his musical instruments, did fiddles of all sizes, and a stringed bass, and at least one lovely 'cello. But there are lots of 'cellos in art, from Thomas Gainsborough to Marc Chagall. And a painting called "Mello Yello Chello" by an artist who loves to do 'cellos, and a 'cellist street sculpture in Houston, Texas.

There are dozens of guitars and violins in art. Giorgioni has a lute in the Venetian pastures, and Rembrandt has a lute or two. Rembrandt should have painted a "Self-Portrait with 'Cello"; and as an old man Degas should have done the dancing-master with his kit-violin and his father sitting on a wooden stool in the background, playing his 'cello.

Thomas Hardy loved the 'cello—though he never really wrote about it. The Mellstock Quire, in *Under the Greenwood Tree,* has its 'cellist, but he isn't an important character. Hardy himself played a 'cello, and you can see his sturdy instrument standing in the corner of his study, still, as that study is reconstructed in the Dorset County Museum in England.

Hardy loved music: it meant something—made *sense*—to him. Michael Henchard, the Mayor of Casterbridge in Hardy's novel by that name, took music seriously. He chose Donald Farfrae as his friend and business manager bcause he heard him singing. Later, when he wanted to kill Farfrae, he couldn't because Farfrae arrived at the point of Henchard's ambush singing. When Henchard wanted to curse Farfrae, he did it by requiring the church choir—after practice, one afternoon—to sing God's curse on David's enemy, in the psalm that ends "And the next age his hated name shall utterly efface."

Hardy loved music enough to attend church regularly, even though he didn't believe in any kind of god. As a young man he played 'cello in the Stinsford choir—with his father and two uncles, on viola and violin. People in Dorchester still recall the now nearly hundred year-old sacrilege—the blasphemy—of the local athiest who, as an old man in his seventies and eighties, used to go to church every Sunday, to hear the music.

All of this about Thomas Hardy because I want to try another tack in my round-about way of talking about the 'cello. Hardy's writings—his novels and his poems—remind me of the 'cello: of the unaccompanied 'cello.

If I try to do Dickens and music I get a full orchestra, with lots of brass and woodwinds and heavy percussion. Everything—every instrument—is there for Dickens, except for bubbly things like xylophones and insincere ones like slide trombones. No French horns, either: English brass.

When you read Dickens you find mention of flutes, pianos, organs. There are violins and fiddles, harps, a 'cello once (in *Bleak House*), drums, and various horns. But Dickens himself is an orchestra: I suspect that that's why he liked the idea of the organ so much—the idea of the one person playing the whole thing. But Dickens's *instrument* can indeed play the whole thing, and do it well. The one-man Dickens orchestra is capable of both the heavy fullness of Beethoven and the total collective transcendence of Mozart. He can write a full but still musical bass rattle, and manage beautifully the romantic elegance of Brahms. And he can also do lots of funny ditties, wicked bits of cutting satire, and delightful sweet little songs in between.

Part of Mozart's genius is that in his music, transcendence isn't what you get from one note, or one phrase: it isn't what a single instrument, rising free, takes you to. For Mozart, transcendence—triumph or tragedy—is what the whole orchestra, the whole piece of music achieves. Listening to Mozart, you almost believe that humanity itself has transcended its limitations.

I remember a sermon at St. Paul's in London, one of Bishop Kenneth Woolcombe's many sermons about Mozart. One summer, when the choir and orchestra were doing the *Coronation Mass* to end the annual Festival of London, he concluded his sermon saying, "Theologians agree that, if there is a heaven, Mozart is there." And if the theologians ever get to heaven they will find, I suspect, that the choirs of angels sing Mozart all day long!

But heaven—if it exists—isn't just for Mozart's sopranos and violins, or the sweet rising harmonies his tenors make together. I will wager confidently that there is a large baritone section in the choir, made up of normal people with human-ranged voices—transformed, certainly and probably dressed a bit differently, but still baritones. And there will be plenty of men and women playing 'cellos in God's heavenly orchestra, too, reminding everybody where they came from. And maybe there will even be a few angels, taking 'cello lessons on the side, trying to find out what being *human* was like.

Thomas Hardy would never do Mozart. He writes traditional English music—and I don't mean by that the tradition of Purcell or Handel and the English court. I mean that traditional *human* strain which plays across the pulses of common life. Hardy's bow plays the strings of the human wrist, interpreting us to ourselves, finding grandeur and even heroism in our little, common lives.

Moreso than any writer I know, Hardy writes like a 'cellist—or, rather, he writes stories and poems that are like the greatest music written for the 'cello.

George Eliot wrote Beethoven symphonies. At her best—in *Middlemarch*—she is just as great as he is. She demonstrates that intellect and intelligence can *move* us. In her work, "feeling is a kind of thought, and thought a kind of feeling": the phrase is hers, describing what she thought the aim and the achievement of all great works of art ought to be.

Jane Austen wrote for the eloquence and wit and moral seriousness of the piano-forte: and the fullness of her genius is more than most of Bach's, but less than Mozart's. Like Bach's, her music lacks the lyricism of Mozart's.

I wonder if Jane Austen knew any of Mozart's music? (She wouldn't have owned a record-player—wouldn't have let one in her house!) If she knew Mozart's music, she must have loved it. At the same time, however, she would probably have objected—in public, anyway—to Mozart's plumage, and to the size of his wings.

Henry James's writing is all strings—mumbling, muttering, endlessly indulging in the chatter of the upper regions of hell. That's not all bad, of course—James is often very good. But if he had written for the 'cello, he would probably have composed for middle-aged baritone grasshoppers, rubbing away in slow sententiousness for hours on end.

Emily Brontë might have written for the 'cello, had she not been addicted to the winds. *Wuthering Heights* is scorecd for oboe, bassoon, serpent, a shrill clarinet, and maybe kettle drums.

There aren't many writers who can write successfully for the 'cello. Turgenev, maybe, in Russian literature—but I'm depending on translations, not reading the Russian. In English literature, Hardy stands out, alone. He knows the range—and he knows how to make, out of singleness, out on one instrument's near simplicity, a *richness* that includes both tension and its resolution. For him, four strings are enough.

In Time of "The Breaking of Nations"

Only a man harrowing clods
In a slow silent walk
With an old horse that stumbles and nods
Half asleep as they stalk.

Only thin smoke without flame
From the heaps of couch-grass:
Yet this will go onward the same
Though Dynasties pass.

Yonder a maid and her wight
Come whispering by:
War's annals will cloud into night
Ere their story die.

That's a poem played quietly, unostentatiously, on the 'cello, in the very unquiet year 1915. Here's another. It starts plainly, but moves toward a rich resonance, a simple and simply stated grandeur.

Transformations

Portion of this yew
Is a man my grandsire knew,
Bosomed here at its foot;
This branch may be his wife,
A ruddy human life,
Now turned to a green shoot.

These grasses must be made
Of her who often prayed
Last century, for repose;
And the fair girl long ago
Whom I often tried to know
May be entering this rose.

So, they are not underground,
But as nerves and veins abound
In the growths of upper air,
And they feel the sun and rain
And the energy again
That made them what they were!

Let me make the argument more directly.

Altos and baritones are never extravagant, never spectacular. You will never hear us breaking fine crystal with the ringing clarity of our high notes, or causing deep vibrations among people's ribs like great basses sometimes do. No. We stand there in the human middle, making music: singing within the range, never tragic, never triumphant or transcendent.

Mozart could do the crystal-breaking, but usually didn't. His genius is always utterly human: the music of *human* glory, of what William Blake called "the human form divine." And thus, though the 'cello's voice is strong and moving in Mozart's trios and quartettes, he never really wrote *for* the 'cello. The 'cello merely accompanied Mozart's genius.

Bach transcended his own limitations—the limitations of his culture, his time, even of his personality—in writing for the 'cello. And in that huge setting of dramatic soliloquies called the "Unaccompanied Suites" he gave the 'cello its greatest role.

Several years ago Yo Yo Ma played Bach at Hill Auditorium in Ann Arbor. The first half of the program consisted of the "Unaccompanied

Suites." I was sitting on the front row, right in the center. I was with Karl Brenner, one of my students. When the music ended, we just sat. Eventually, after the applause had died out, people around us began to move. We didn't. For a long time we didn't say anything—just sat. Finally Karl said, without looking at me or even seeming to speak to me, "I feel like I've been turned inside out."

He didn't say he felt transported, or carried away. No. Turned inside-out.

The "Unaccompanied Suites" are the greatest achievements of Bach's career. In them he opens himself up to the dangerous freedom of unsecured emotion. It is not that his 'cello extends itself, finds new notes to play in the distant ranges of possibility or impossibility. The "Unaccompanied Suites" are not virtuoso compositions. If you have heard Yo Yo Ma perform them, you understand from the very brilliance of the performance that they are not virtuoso pieces. Their brilliance resides in the eloquence of the human voice—the 'cello's *own* voice—exploring the rich and varied reality of this existence, this moving little life. There is no need for what we call "transcendence." Staying right here is more than enough.

Beethoven's 'cello is always a reminder of our limitations. It is beautiful in what it says, but it plays—like the left hand in the hammer-klavier sonata—to recall us to our humanity, to refuse transcendence. It doesn't stand alone; it *answers* our larger ambitions, spoken by the violin. It plays the heavy, retarding the violin's follow-the-leader flight.

Brahms lets the 'cello sing again. And in the great double concerto, under the influence of its violin companion, the 'cello almost exceeds itself without ceasing to be itself. His careful, conservative romanticism lets the lovely, delicate, tender violin lead the 'cello to sing with a new eloquence. It is one of us, accompanying an angel. The baritone voice keeps reaching up, up, not in head-tones, but somehow still resonantly baritone, still two-legged and winglessly human.

Human.

One of the sweetest of great humans is the wonderful old hero of Anthony Trollope's Barchester novels, the reverend Septimus Harding. Mr. Harding—"a good man without guile," Trollope calls him—has played his 'cello most of his life, and has found great human comfort in it. Indeed, he finds such comfort in his 'cello that, under stress, Mr. Harding is wont to play it in his imagination. He has "an old trick," Trollope writes, that is "customary to him" when he is sad, or disturbed: he plays "some slow tune upon an imaginmary violincello, drawing one hand slowly backwards and forwards as though he held a bow in it, and modulating the unreal chords with the other."

As he approaches death, Mr. Harding can no longer play. He is no longer strong enough even to hold his 'cello. But sometimes, when there is no one near to see him but Trollope, he still opens the case of his 'cello, and sometimes he even plucks an untuned string.

In several different scenes, Trollope proposes to us the connection between Mr. Harding's 'cello and his life: it is the mirror of his humanity. And it is Mr. Harding's humanity which Trollope celebrates, quietly, throughout his *Chronicles of Barset.*

In a world in which sermons are always either flaccidly moral or belligerently political, the reverend Mr. Harding's playing his 'cello is the most decent thing—the one truly religious and spiritual and uplifting and genuine thing—that we hear.

While others talk of God or assert self—or confuse those two as one—Mr. Harding speaks, ever so quietly, with his 'cello. And the voice of his 'cello, even when the bow and the 'cello are both but part of Mr. Harding's dream, both only imagined: the voice of his 'cello is the truly heroic voice of decent humanity.

If we want to learn what God is—or heaven, or the beatific vision—perhaps we should listen to the violin, on the upper ranges of the harp, or the ice-breaking perfection of a great soprano. And if we want to know the depths which exceed our normal human experience, and shake us even in our bones, we can listen to the dramatic basses of the variously rumbling kinds—or the deep, tone-swallowing, stone-rattling noises big pipe organs can make.

But to learn of human life—to discover, perhaps, the real or at least the possible beauty of our own little existences—to hear the rich, lovely comedy as well as the poignantly human tragedy (and there *is* no tragedy but human tragedy)—we must listen to the baritone.

And all baritones tend toward, honor, proclaim, bless, and would imitate—if they could—the 'cello.

And oh, we say: oh, to be a 'cello!

Words that Sing

1. A DRINKING SONG

2. THE LAKE ISLE OF INSIFREE
W. B. YEATS
I will a- rise and go now, and go to In- is- free, and a
small ca- bin build there, of clay and watt- les made:
Nine bean rows will I have there, a hive for the ho- ney- bee, and
live a- lone in the bee- loud glade. And I shall have some
peace there, for peace comes drop- ping slow, drop- ping from the

11
3
3
12
veils of morn to where the cri cket sings;
There mid- night's all a-
3
13
14
glim- mer,
and noon a purp- le
glow,
and eve- ning full of the
15
3
16
lin- net's wings.
I will
arise and go now,
for al- ways
3
17
18
night and day
I hear lake
wa- ter lap- ping,
with low sound
19
3
20
by the shore;
while I stand
on the road- way,
or on the
3

21
22
3
pave- ment grey, I hear it
in the deep heart's core.
3

3. BROWN PENNY

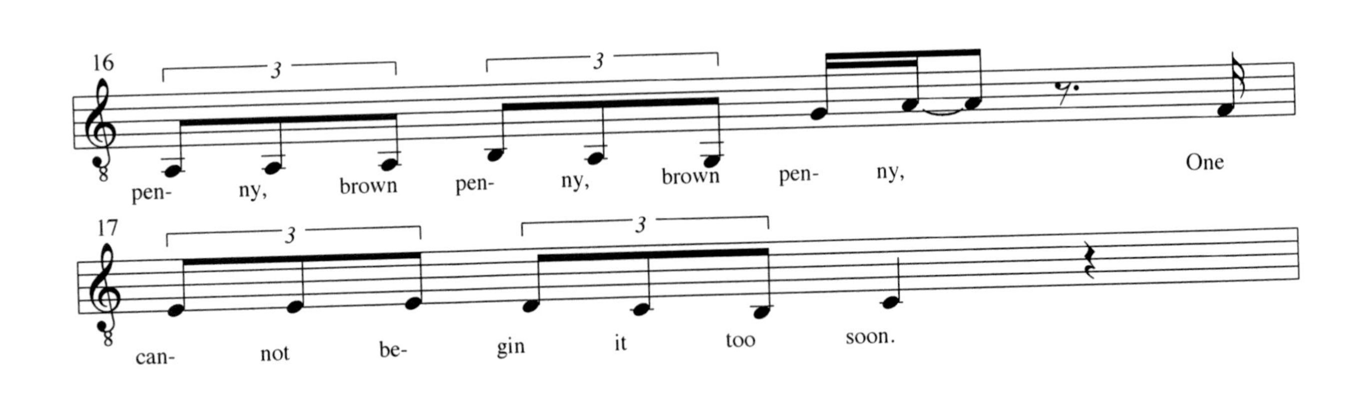
16
3
3
pen- ny, brown pen- ny, brown pen- ny, One
17
3
3
can- not be- gin it too soon.

4. THE FIDDLER OF DOONAY

17 18 19
fair. When we come at the end of time To
20 21 22
Pe- ter sit- ting in state, He will smile on the three old
23 24 25
spi- rits, But call me first through the gate; For the
26 27 28 29
good are al- ways the mer- ry, Save by an e- vil chance, And the
30 31 32
mer- ry love the fid- dle, And the mer- ry love to

33
34
35
dance: And when the folk there spy me, They will
36
37
38
39
all come up to me, With 'Here is the fidd- ler of Doo- nay!' And
40
41
42
dance like a wave of the sea. And dance like a wave of the
43
44
45
s- e- a, And dance like a wave of the sea.

5. SEA FEVER

JOHN MASEFIELD

6. THE JABBERWOCKY

16
Jab- ber- wock, with eyes of flame, Came
17
whiff- ling through the tul- gey wood, and
18
bur- bled as it came! One,
19
two! One, two! And through and through the
20
3
vor- pal blade went snick- er- snack! He
21
22
left it dead, and with its head he went ga- lum- phing back. "And
23
hast thou slain the Jab- ber- wock?
24
3
Come to my arms, my beam- ish boy! O
25
3
26
frab- jous day! Cal- lo- oh! Cal- lay!" he chort- led in his joy.
27
3
28
'Twas brillig, and the sli- thy tove did gyre and gim- ble
29
30
in the wabe; All mim- sy were the bo- ro- grove,

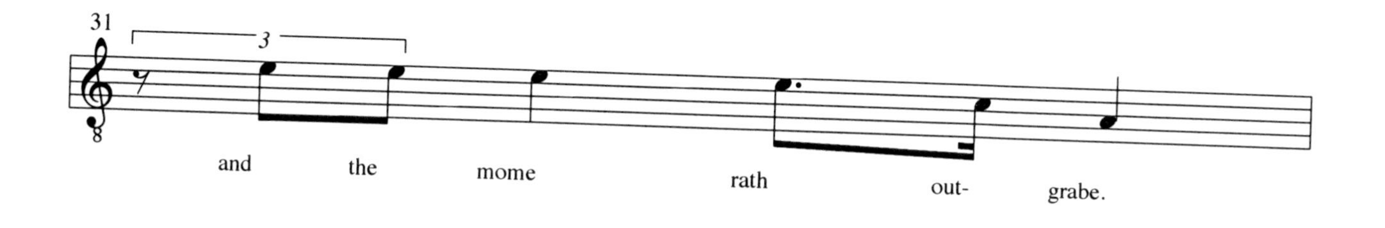
31
3
and the mome rath out- grabe.

7. SONG

JOHN DONNE

8. BREAK, BREAK, BREAK

34
35
36
37
38
39
40
ships go on To their ha- ven un- der the hill; But
41
42
43
44
45
O for the touch of a va- nish'd hand, And the sound of a
46
47
48
49
50
51
52
53
voice that's still! Break, break, break, At the foot of thy
54
55
56
57
58
59
crags, O sea! But the ten- der grace of a day that's
60
61
62
63
64
dead Will ne- ver come back to me.

9. IN TIME OF 'THE BREAKING OF NATIONS'

THOMAS HARDY

10. TO AN UNBORN PAUPER CHILD

THOMAS HARDY

21
22
tell thee all I know, And put it to thee: Wilt thou take life
23
24
so? Vain vow! No hint of mine may
25
26
hence To thee- ward fly: to thy locked sense Ex- plain none
27
28
can Life's pen- ding plan: Thou wilt thy ig- no- rant
29
30
en- try make Thou skies spout fire and blood and na- tions
31
32
quake. Fain would I, dear, find some shut
33
34
plot Of earth's wide wold for thee, where not One tear, one
35
36
qualm, Should break the calm. But I am weak as thou and bare;
37
38
No man can change the com- mon lot to rare. Must
39
40
41
come and bide. And such are we -- Un- rea- son- ing, san- guine, vi- sion-

42
43
44
ary --
That I can hope Health, love, friends, scope In full for
45
46
thee: can dream thoul't find Joys sel- dom yet at- tained by
47
hu- man- kind!

11. ODE: INTIMATIONS OF IMMORTALITY
WILLIAM WORDSWORTH
There was a time when me- dow, grove, and stream, The
earth and eve- ry com- mon sight to me did seem Ap- pare- led
in ce- les- tial light, The glo- ry and the fresh- ness of a dream.
It is not now as it hath been be- fore; Turn where- so-

17
18
19
20
e'er I may, By
night or day,
The things which
I have seen
21
22
23
24
25
I now can
see no more.
The
rain- bow comes and
goes and
26
27
28
29
love- ly is the
rose, The
moon doth with de-
light look round her
30
31
32
33
when the heavens are
bare;
Wa- ters on a
sum- mer night are

34
35
36
37
38
beau- ti- ful and fair.
The sun- shine is a glo- rious birth;
39
40
41
42
But yet I know where- e'er I go That there hath passed a-
43
44
45
46
way a glo- ry from the earth.
Now while the birds thus sing a
47
48
49
50
joy- ous song,
And while the young lambs bound
to the ta- bor's

51
52
53
54
sound, To me a- lone there came a thought of grief; A time- ly
55
56
57
58
utter- ance gave that thought re- lief, And I a- gain am strong:
59
60
61
62
The cata- racts blow their trum- pets from the steep; No
63
64
65
66
more shall grief of mine the sea- son wrong. I hear the e- choes

67
68
69
through the moun- tains throng, the winds come to me
70
71
72
73
through the fields of sleep. And all the earth is gay;
74
75
76
77
Land and sea give them- selves up to jol- li- ty, And
78
79
80
81
with the heart of May Doth eve- ry beast keep ho- li- day; Thou

82
83
84
85
child of joy, Shout round me, let me hear thy shouts Thou
86
87
88
89
hap- py shep- herd boy. Ye bles- sed crea- tures, I have
90
91
92
93
heard the call Ye to each o- ther make; I see the hea- vens
94
95
96
Laugh with you in your ju- bi- lee; My heart's at your

97
98
99
100
fes- ti- val, My head hath its co- ro- nal, The full- ness of your
101
102
103
104
105
106
bliss -- I feel, I feel it all! But there's a tree,
107
108
109
110
of ma- ny, one; a sing- le field which I have looked up-
111
112
113
114
on; Both of them speak of some- thing that is gone. The

115
116
117
118
pan- sy at my feet Doth the same tale re- peat: Whi- ther is
119
120
121
122
fled the vi- sio- na- ry gleam? Where is it now, the
123
124
125
126
127
glo- ry and the dream? Our birth is but a sleep and a for-
128
129
130
131
get- ting: The soul that ri- ses with us, our life's star Hath

132
133
134
135
had else- where its set- ting, and co- meth from a- far, Not
136
137
138
139
in en- tire for- get- ful- ness, And not in ut- ter na- ked- ness But
140
141
142
143
trail -ing clouds of glo- ry do we come From God who is our
144
145
146
147
home. Hea- ven lies a- bout us in our in- fan- cy;

148
149
150
Shades of the pri- son house be- gin to close Up-
151
152
153
on the grow- ing boy, But he be- holds the
154
155
156
157
light, and whence it flows. He sees it in his joy. The
158
159
160
youth, who dai- ly far- ther from the east Must tra- vel,

161
162
163
164
still is na- ture's priest, And by the vi- sion splen- did Is
165
166
167
168
on his way at- tend- ed; At length the man per- ceives it die a-
169
170
171
172
173
way, And fade in- to the light of com- mon day. Earth
174
175
176
177
fills her lap with plea- sures of her own: Year- nings she hath in

178
179
180
her own natu- ral kind, And, e- ven with some- thing
181
182
183
184
of a mo- ther's mind, And no un- worth- y aim. The
185
186
187
home- ly nurse doth all she can To make her fos- ter-
188
189
190
191
child, her in- mate man, For- get the glo- ries he hath

192
193
194
195
196
known, And that im- peri- al pa- lace whence he came. Migh- ty
197
198
199
200
201
pro- phet! Se- er blest! On whom these truths do rest, Thou
202
203
204
205
eye a- mong the blind: Thou lit- tle child, yet
206
207
208
209
glo- rious in thy might: Full soon thy soul will have her earth- ly

210
211
212
213
freight, and cus- tom lie up- on thee with a weight,
214
215
216
217
Hea- vy as frost, and deep al- most as life! O
218
219
220
221
joy! That in our em- bers Is some- thing that doth live, That
222
223
224
225
226
Na- ture yet re- mem- bers What was so fu- gi- tive! Then

227
228
229
230
sing, ye birds! sing a joy- ous song! And let the young lambs bound
231
232
233
234
to the ta- bor's sound! We in thought will join your throng,
235
236
237
238
Ye that pipe and ye that play, Ye that through your hearts to- day
239
240
241
242
Feel the glad- ness of the May! What though the ra- diance

243
244
245
246
which was once so bright Be now for- ev- er ta- ken from my
247
248
249
250
sight, Though no- thing can bring back the hour Of splen- dour in the
251
252
253
254
255
grass, of glo- ry in the flower; We will grieve not, ra- ther find
256
257
258
Strength in what re- mains be- hind; In the pri- mal

259
260
261
262
sym- pa- thy Which ha- ving been must e- ver be; In the
263
264
265
266
sooth- ing thoughts that spring out of hu- man suf- fer- ing;
267
268
269
In the faith that looks through death, In years that bring the
270
271
272
273
phi- lo- soph- ic mind. And oh, ye foun- tains,

274
275
276
277
mea- dows, hills, and groves, Fore- bode not a- ny sever- ing of our
278
279
280
281
loves! Yet in my heart of hearts I feel your might; I
282
283
284
285
on- ly have re- lin- quished one de- light: To live be- neath your
286
287
288
289
more ha- bi- tual sway. I love the brooks which down their chan- nels

290
291
292
293
fret E- ven more than when I tripped light- ly as they; The
294
295
296
297
in- no- cent bright- ness of a new- born day Is love- ly yet; An-
298
299
300
301
302
oth- er race hath been, and o- ther palms are won. Thanks
303
304
305
306
to the hu- man heart by which we live, Thanks to its ten- der-

307
308
309
310
ness, its joys, its
fears, To
me the mea- nest
flower that blows can
311
312
313
314
give Thoughts
that do of- ten
lie too deep for
tears.

12. A CLASSICAL ROUND
BERT HORNBACK
Jo- hann Se- ba- sti- an Ba- ach
Jo- hann Se- ba- sti- an Ba- ach
Wolf- gang A- ma- de- us Mo- zart
Wolf- gang A- ma- de- us Mo- zart
Jo- han- nes Brahms
Jo- han- nes Brahms
Lud- wig van Beet- ho- ven
Lud- wig van Beet- ho- ven

13. ODE ON AN EXPIRING FROG, BY MRS. LEO HUNTER

from THE PICKWICK PAPERS, by CHARLES DICKENS

CPSIA information can be obtained
at www.ICGtesting.com
Printed in the USA
FFOW04n0828290615
14673FF

9 781629 0121